Winds of the Silent Hills
Biswajit Paria

Copyright © 2024 Biswajit Paria

This is a work of fiction. Names, characters, businesses, places, events, and incidents are either the product of the author's imagination or used in a fictitious manner. Any resemblance to actual persons, living or dead, or actual events is purely coincidental.

All rights reserved. No part of this book may be reproduced, distributed, or transmitted in any form or by any means, including photocopying, recording, or other electronic or mechanical methods, without the prior written permission of the publisher.

Dedication

To my wife Payel and daughter Titli—your love is the heartbeat of my life. This book is for you both, with all my gratitude.

Table of Contents

Prologue
    Chapter 1: **Refuge in the Mountains**
  Chapter 2: **Storm Warnings**
  Chapter 3: **The Approach**
  Chapter 4: **Into the Mist**
  Chapter 5: **Trust Amid Danger**
  Chapter 6: **A New Beginning**
  Chapter 7: **Rising Shadows**
  Chapter 8: **Storm of Ghosts**
  Chapter 9: **Shadows of Thunder**
  Chapter 10: **The Gathering Storm**
  Chapter 11: **The Tempest's Fury**
  Chapter 12: **Shadows of Sacrifice**
Epilogue

Prologue

The storm that had once gripped the desert outside Cairo felt like a half-remembered nightmare, a fierce and unforgiving struggle that had left scars both seen and unseen. Isabella and Bijoy had survived that tempest, escaped Rahim al-Zahir's relentless pursuit, and traversed the perilous sands to the safety of Alexandria. But the memories of that night, the crackling lightning and swirling sands, had marked the beginning of something far greater than either could have anticipated.

Now, in the quietude of dawn in Calcutta, Isabella stood by an open window, the scent of rain-slicked earth mingling with the faint aroma of the morning's first chai stalls. She traced the edge of the silver medallion at her neck—an artifact that had guided them through more than just storms of sand. It had been a silent witness to their victories and losses, a reminder of the journeys that had brought them here.

Beside her, Bijoy sat with Pluto resting at his feet, the dog's dark eyes glancing up now and then as if he could sense the unrest in the room. They had faced their share of perils in Cairo, from labyrinthine alleys to the treacherous alleys of Rahim's spies. They had uncovered artifacts that whispered of ancient powers and kingdoms lost to time, relics that spoke of a resistance buried deep in the sands and histories untold.

But now, Calcutta simmered with its own turmoil. The whispers in the city were no longer of ancient secrets but of rebellion, the air thick with the tension of a population ready to rise. The British had grown wary, their hold on the city turning tighter, suffocating the spirit of freedom that pulsed just beneath the surface.

Isabella's fingers tightened around the medallion, its cool surface pressing into her palm as if to remind her of its unspoken promises. The memories of their flight across the desert, Bijoy's steady hand guiding her through impossible odds, returned with vivid clarity. That night had not only been a fight for survival but a pledge, unspoken and sealed by the shifting sands, that they would stand together against whatever storm came next.

"Isabella," Bijoy's voice interrupted her reverie, drawing her eyes to his. His face, lined with exhaustion, still held the strength she had come to rely on. "The city is changing. The resistance grows restless, and soon it will no longer be whispers but shouts."

She nodded, a spark of determination igniting in her chest. The medallion caught the morning light, casting a flicker of silver onto the wall—a ghostly reminder that even here, in the shadow of rebellion, they were not alone.

"I know," she said, her voice steady. "The winds are shifting, and we need to be ready when they do."

Pluto's ears twitched as a distant echo of shouts reached them, voices carried by the wind from the heart of the city. Bijoy stood, moving to the window, his hand finding hers as they watched the streets below stir with the early rise of the city.

WINDS OF THE SILENT HILLS

The path that had brought them from Cairo to Calcutta had been marked by hidden alliances and fragile hopes. It was in the hidden markets of Cairo where the *Silent Messenger*—a network of informants and rebels—had first led them to the medallion and the artifacts that spoke of a history long concealed. Now, as the dawn light revealed the restless streets of Calcutta, the echoes of that past whispered promises of more battles to come.

"Do you think we can do it?" Bijoy asked quietly, his eyes still on the horizon.

She turned to him, the weight of the medallion warm against her chest, a reminder of that shared night in the storm, of their survival against the odds. "We have to," she replied. "The winds are restless, and they're bringing us to the silent hills."

Bijoy glanced at her, understanding in his eyes. He nodded, a silent agreement that their journey was far from over. The past had marked them, and the future would call for everything they had gained, every lesson learned in Cairo, every bond forged in the shadow of danger.

As they stood there, the shouts from the city grew louder, joined by the distant clamor of marching feet. The storm they had once faced in the desert had passed, but a new storm was brewing, one that would not be confined to the shifting sands but would echo across the silent hills and beyond. And as the wind carried the scent of rain and unrest, Isabella and Bijoy knew that their adventure was only just beginning.

Chapter 1: Refuge in the Mountains

Calcutta was alive with unrest, its humid air laced with smoke, fear, and anticipation. Once the jewel of British India, the city now writhed in pain, burdened with its own desire for freedom. In every alley and shadowed street, whispers of revolt lingered. Bijoy could feel the weight of it, pressing against his skin like the heavy clouds overhead, which seemed ready to burst with a storm. Rain would have been a welcome relief from the suffocating heat and smoke, yet none came. Only thunder rolled ominously over the city, echoing the gunfire and cries in the distance.

Standing at Howrah Station, Bijoy held tightly to the leash of Pluto, his loyal black-and-white dog. The mutt looked around with a keen intelligence, ears perked, his stance alert as if sensing the urgency in his master's movements. Beside them, Isabella's face was pale, her eyes wide as she took in the chaotic scene at the station. Pluto pressed close to her leg, offering silent comfort.

"We don't have much time," Bijoy murmured, casting a nervous glance down the platform. The air was thick with smoke from the smoldering city, mingling with the smell of sweat and fear that clung to the crowds around them. The faint shrill of a train whistle pierced the thick atmosphere—a reminder that their escape was waiting.

Pluto whined softly, nudging Bijoy's leg, as if urging him to hurry.

Bijoy tightened his grip on Isabella's hand. "We're almost there," he said, trying to sound confident. But he knew the truth. Calcutta was no longer a place for people like them, people who dared to think beyond what the British allowed. Even now, he could feel eyes on him, every uniformed soldier a potential threat.

Finally, the train rolled in, its massive iron form shrouded in steam as it slowed to a stop. Bijoy took a deep breath, a mixture of hope and fear rising in him. They were really doing it—they were leaving everything behind.

As they climbed aboard, Pluto trotted ahead, his tail high but his ears back, scanning their surroundings as if assessing the danger himself. They found their seats near a grimy window, and as Bijoy sat down, he couldn't resist one last look at the city. The once-familiar skyline of Calcutta was blurred now, shrouded in smoke and hazy evening light, making it look ghostly, as if the place itself was fading from memory.

"Bijoy, are you all right?" Isabella's voice was soft, her hand resting gently on his arm.

He managed a nod, but his voice faltered. "I never thought it would come to this. Leaving... as if we're being driven out by our own city."

Isabella looked out the window, a shadow passing over her face. "It's not the same Calcutta we loved. It's not home anymore."

She was right, though the truth of it stung. Bijoy felt Pluto's head nudge his hand, and he gave the dog a quick scratch behind the ears, feeling the comforting warmth of the creature's presence. Pluto, as always, seemed to understand the gravity of their situation, sitting with his body tensed, his brown eyes fixed on Bijoy as if waiting for a command.

The train shuddered, lurching forward with a jolt that made Isabella gasp. Outside, the station platform began to slide away, the city receding like a dream they were waking from. Bijoy and Isabella held hands, fingers intertwined, while Pluto settled beside them, his head resting on his paws but his eyes ever-watchful.

The railcars creaked and groaned as they picked up speed, the wheels rattling loudly over the iron tracks. For the first hour, they passed through the outskirts of Calcutta, a place where buildings were less grand but still familiar, reminders of the life they were leaving. Bijoy couldn't look away, his eyes fixed on the city he loved, despite everything.

"Think we'll find peace in Ghum?" Isabella asked, her voice low.

Bijoy sighed, his gaze dropping to their entwined hands. "That's what I'm hoping for." He glanced down at Pluto. "It'll be quieter, at least. For us, and for him."

Isabella managed a small smile. "A quiet life sounds... like something I've forgotten how to imagine."

The cityscape gave way to the vast, green plains stretching toward the horizon, dotted with rice paddies and small farms. The train continued to rumble northward, the flat plains soon shifting to rolling hills cloaked in a thickening mist. The clouds hung low and heavy, blanketing the fields in a gray, muted light that added to the somber mood of the passengers.

The rain began as a soft drizzle, the drops streaking against the windows in steady lines, gathering and rolling down in rivulets. The dim light inside the carriage flickered, casting shadows that danced across the faces of the few other travelers, silent figures lost in their own worlds.

Pluto lifted his head, his ears twitching as he watched the raindrops on the glass. Bijoy followed his gaze, his own thoughts drifting into silence, the tension easing slightly as the monotony of the journey set in.

But the quiet was deceptive. A deep foreboding settled over him, as if the misty hills beyond the window held secrets of their own. He glanced over at Isabella, noting the worry etched into her face.

She must have felt his gaze, because she turned to him and whispered, "Do you think... do you think we'll be safe?"

He wanted to reassure her, to say that Ghum would be far enough, remote enough. But a part of him knew that Calcutta had a way of leaving its mark. And as long as the war raged, no place was truly safe. "As safe as we can be," he replied. "We'll keep low, stay quiet. It's a small town... no one will be looking for us there."

Pluto gave a low growl, his hackles rising as he looked toward the window. Bijoy followed his gaze, but there was only the darkening landscape beyond, swallowed by the mist. He reached down to pat the dog's head, hoping to calm him, though his own unease grew.

The hours passed slowly. Outside, the drizzle turned to a steady downpour, hammering against the roof and windows with relentless fury. The mist thickened until the landscape was little more than shadows in the rain. Shadows that seemed to move, ghostly shapes darting across fields and paths before vanishing back into the fog.

Bijoy dozed fitfully, lulled by the clacking of the train. In his dreams, he was back in Calcutta, running through the streets, always looking over his shoulder, always just one step ahead of something he couldn't see. He heard the shouts, the roar of crowds, the pounding of boots on cobblestones... and a howl, piercing the din like a blade.

"Bijoy!"

Isabella's voice jolted him awake, her hand tight on his arm. He looked around, disoriented, as the rain continued to lash the window. Pluto was standing, his body stiff, his ears flattened, teeth bared in a low, warning growl.

"What is it?" he asked, his voice hoarse from sleep.

Isabella shook her head, her face pale. "I thought I saw something... someone... on the tracks. But it must have been the rain."

Pluto growled again, his eyes fixed on the window, refusing to relax. Bijoy felt a chill run down his spine as he followed the dog's gaze. There was nothing out there, only rain and shadow. But the unease gnawed at him, a feeling he couldn't shake.

The train clattered through the night, winding up into the mountains as they left the plains behind. The journey seemed endless, time losing all meaning in the gloom. Every now and then, Bijoy glanced down at Pluto, who remained vigilant, his eyes trained on the darkness outside.

Near dawn, the train finally slowed, its whistle echoing through the mountains like a lonely cry. They had arrived in Ghum.

As they stepped off the train, the chill of the mountain air struck them, the damp mist clinging to their skin like a second layer. Pluto trotted alongside, his nose to the ground, sniffing the unfamiliar scents, his stance alert yet curious.

The station was little more than a solitary wooden platform, aged and worn, surrounded by looming trees and thick fog that seemed almost alive, swirling in endless patterns. Bijoy scanned the area, taking in the quiet stillness, so different from the city. Isabella clutched his arm, her eyes scanning the fog.

"This place... it's like stepping into another world," she murmured, shivering.

They made their way toward the village center, the narrow path winding through the trees. Shadows flitted at the edges of their vision, shapes barely visible in the mist, making every step feel like a walk through a haunted dream. Pluto seemed to sense something too, his gaze darting from tree to tree, his hackles raised slightly.

Finally, they reached their small, rented cottage on the outskirts of the village. It was an old structure, half-hidden by ivy and trees, its wooden walls darkened by years of rain and mist. The door creaked as Bijoy pushed it open, revealing a dim interior lit only by the faint gray of early dawn.

Pluto entered first, sniffing around the room with an air of cautious authority, as though verifying that it was truly safe. Bijoy and Isabella followed, their breaths visible in the cold air. The room was simple, furnished with a few chairs, a table, and an old clay stove, all cloaked in dust and the lingering smell of damp wood.

"It's... not much, but it's ours," Bijoy said, his voice thick with a mixture of exhaustion and relief.

Isabella managed a tired smile. "It's perfect."

Pluto finally settled near the doorway, still keeping an eye on the fog-shrouded world outside. Bijoy crouched beside him, running a hand over his fur. "You're going to keep us safe, aren't you, boy?"

The dog looked up at him, his eyes bright and unwavering. In that moment, Bijoy felt a surge of gratitude for the animal's unwavering loyalty, knowing that, no matter what lay ahead, they wouldn't face it alone.

As the rain continued to fall outside, the small cottage grew quiet, wrapped in shadows and silence. But as Bijoy and Isabella settled into their new home, a feeling of unease lingered. Beyond the fog-shrouded mountains, the fires of rebellion still burned, and though they had found temporary shelter, something in the mist seemed to watch them, waiting for the right moment to step into the light.

Chapter 2: Storm Warnings

Inside the small cottage, Bijoy and Isabella huddled near the fire as the storm clawed at their walls. Their German Shepherd, Pluto, lay at their feet, his ears twitching each time thunder rumbled outside. The room flickered with shadows cast by the firelight, giving the space an almost haunted feeling, as though ghosts lurked in the corners, waiting for a break in the silence.

Isabella traced small circles on Bijoy's hand, her fingers cold against his warm skin. They had taken refuge in this remote mountain village to escape the life they'd left behind in Calcutta, and yet something about the night—the wildness of the storm, the unsettling emptiness of the valley, and even the thick silence between them—felt like an omen.

"You're thinking about it too, aren't you?" she murmured, her voice barely louder than the rain.

Bijoy tightened his grip on her hand, giving a silent nod. He didn't need to say what was on his mind; they had been together long enough that words were often unnecessary. They had taken a risk in coming to Ghum, a remote village forgotten by most and hidden from the maps. It was supposed to be their sanctuary—a place to forget, to heal. But some shadows couldn't be left behind.

Pluto let out a low growl, his head lifting toward the door as another gust of wind howled through the trees. Isabella stroked his head, feeling the warmth of his fur against her chilled fingers.

"You sense it too, don't you, boy?" she whispered. Pluto's ears flattened as he looked toward the door, his hackles raised slightly.

"Strange night," Bijoy said, watching the flames lick up toward the stone chimney. "It's as if the mountains themselves are restless."

Isabella looked at him, her expression haunted. "Do you think we're really safe here?"

Bijoy gave her a reassuring squeeze. "As safe as we can be," he said, but even he didn't seem entirely convinced. The storm rattled the windows again, and a crack of lightning split the sky, illuminating the empty valley outside, then fading just as quickly.

For a while, they sat in silence, the only sounds the rhythmic patter of rain and the occasional crackle of the fire. It was a moment of fragile peace—a brief escape from the memories that haunted them. But in a single instant, that peace shattered.

There was a sharp knock at the door—three loud, insistent raps that seemed to echo above the storm. Bijoy stiffened, exchanging a worried glance with Isabella. Outside, Pluto sprang to his feet, his growl turning into a deep, menacing bark as he stood protectively in front of the door, his body rigid.

"Who could that be at this hour?" Isabella asked, her voice barely a whisper, fear edging into her tone.

Bijoy rose, gesturing for her to stay back as he approached the door. Pluto stayed close, his bark turning into a low, guttural growl, teeth bared as his hackles bristled. Bijoy glanced through the peephole and exhaled sharply.

"It's Satya," he said, his voice edged with relief but also concern. He opened the door, and Inspector Satya stumbled inside, drenched from head to toe, rainwater streaming from his coat and pooling on the wooden floor. His face was pale, eyes wide with something far beyond exhaustion.

"Satya!" Isabella's voice was tense. "What happened?"

The inspector shook off his coat, his hands trembling as he set a dripping lantern down on the table. He exchanged a grim look with Bijoy, his mouth set in a thin line.

"They've found us," he said, the words heavy with dread. "The Order of the Horizon... they're here."

The words hung in the air like a curse. Isabella felt her stomach drop, the shadows closing in around her. They had fought for so long against this secret society, a powerful organization that lurked in the underworld of Calcutta and beyond, weaving webs of influence that spanned entire regions. They had thought they'd escaped—had hoped that Ghum would be far enough, remote enough. But there were no lengths to which the Order wouldn't go, no corners of the earth they couldn't reach.

Pluto whimpered, sensing the tension, and nuzzled against Bijoy's leg. Bijoy gave him a brief pat, as if seeking his own courage from the loyal animal.

"Are you certain?" Bijoy's voice was tense, already preparing for the worst.

"Absolutely," Satya replied, his gaze flicking to the rain-soaked windows as if expecting someone to appear in the storm at any moment. "They've set up operations in the old manor on the outskirts of the village. I've seen their symbols. Their men. This isn't a coincidence—they're here, and they're planning something."

Bijoy clenched his fists, a mixture of fear and anger settling over his face. "How long have they been here?"

"Long enough to establish themselves," Satya replied grimly. "The manor has been under heavy surveillance—armed guards, and they've installed security systems. They don't want anyone snooping around."

Bijoy's eyes darkened, memories from Calcutta rising like specters from the past. "What are they doing here, exactly?"

Satya cast a wary glance toward Isabella, his tone heavy. "Smuggling. Coercion. Possibly worse. Whatever they're involved in, it's big—and they're covering their tracks well. This isn't the kind of operation they set up unless there's something extremely valuable at stake."

Bijoy shared a look with Isabella, whose face had drained of color. She was painfully familiar with the Order's tactics, their cruelty. It wasn't just about money with them; it was about control. Secrets. The hidden power they could wield over others.

"What do they want here?" she asked, her voice barely a whisper.

Satya's eyes grew colder. "I don't know yet, but there are whispers of something more dangerous than what we dealt with in Calcutta. There's talk of... artifacts. Rituals." He paused, a flicker of unease breaking through his usual stoic expression.

"Something ancient. Something the Order believes could grant them... abilities."

Pluto let out a sharp bark, pacing restlessly at Bijoy's side. Isabella's heart clenched. She'd always dismissed such talk as myth, superstition. But the Order had proven time and again that they thrived on the darker fringes of society—on fear and manipulation. She looked at Bijoy, her jaw set.

"We need to stop them," she said, a fierce determination sparking in her eyes. "This is our home now. If they take control here, they won't stop until they control everyone."

Bijoy placed a steadying hand on her shoulder. "We'll stop them, Isa. But we need to be smart. If we go in unprepared..."

Satya cut in. "You'll be slaughtered. The manor is guarded like a fortress. They have lookouts posted, and there's no telling how many of their men are inside. If we're going to do this, we need to gather information first."

"Is there any way inside?" Bijoy asked.

Satya shook his head. "Not directly. But there's a vantage point just behind the manor, hidden by the forest. From there, we might be able to observe them without being seen. And," he added, glancing down at Pluto, "a certain stealthy companion might be able to get close enough to catch their scent."

Bijoy knelt beside Pluto, rubbing the dog's ears as he looked him in the eye. "How about it, boy? You up for a little spying?"

Pluto wagged his tail, letting out a bark as if in agreement. Isabella watched, a slight smile breaking through her worry. She knew Pluto was more than capable—his loyalty was unmatched, and he'd been Bijoy's constant companion through all their ordeals. If anyone could move silently and remain unnoticed, it was Pluto.

"Then it's settled," Satya said, glancing between them. "We go tomorrow night. We'll watch from the forest, document their movements, and see if we can learn anything useful. If we're lucky, we might catch a break."

They spent the rest of the night planning, mapping out every possible detail until the fire had dwindled to embers and the first light of dawn broke through the rain-streaked windows. The storm had quieted, leaving the valley cloaked in mist, the trees heavy with dew. Exhausted but resolute, they retreated to separate corners of the cottage to rest.

The following night arrived with a creeping chill. The storm had left the air thick and damp, and a low fog clung to the forest, obscuring their path as they crept through the trees toward the manor. Pluto walked close beside Bijoy, his body low to the ground, every sense on high alert.

Ahead, the manor loomed—a massive, decaying structure shrouded in darkness, its windows like empty eyes watching the forest. From their vantage point, they could see guards patrolling the perimeter, lanterns in hand, their shadows stretching long across the wet ground.

They settled behind a thicket of trees, crouching low as they surveyed the manor. The guards moved with precision, each taking careful steps as if trained soldiers. Bijoy tightened his grip on Pluto's collar, holding the dog back as he watched for any sign of an opening.

An hour passed. Then another. Just as they began to think they'd see nothing, a carriage rolled up to the front gates, its wheels creaking through the silence. The guards parted, and the gates opened, admitting the vehicle with an air of reverence. Three men emerged from the carriage, each wearing dark, hooded cloaks adorned with strange symbols—markings that made Isabella's blood run cold.

Pluto let out a low growl, his body rigid beside Bijoy. He scratched at the earth, his gaze fixed on the cloaked men as they entered the manor.

"Good boy," Bijoy whispered, calming him with a gentle touch. He glanced at Isabella, who had gone pale, her eyes fixed on the strange symbols on the men's cloaks. These were no ordinary men—they were part of the Order, men who wielded power like a weapon.

The group watched as the doors to the manor closed, leaving the guards to resume their positions around the perimeter. Their mission tonight was only reconnaissance, yet a creeping dread told Isabella that the Order was planning something far darker than she'd imagined.

Bijoy gave her hand a reassuring squeeze. "We'll figure it out," he whispered. "And whatever they're planning... we'll stop them."

She looked at him, her expression fierce despite the fear in her eyes. "I'm with you, Bijoy. Whatever it takes."

They melted back into the shadows, retreating through the forest with Pluto leading the way, his senses sharp as he guided them safely home. Their steps were silent, but the warning hung heavy in the air around them, mingling with the lingering storm as they prepared for the battle ahead.

Chapter 3: The Approach

Bijoy led the way, moving stealthily over the damp, snow-speckled ground. Pluto, his loyal German Shepherd, stayed close at his side, his eyes sharp and alert, occasionally glancing up at his master for silent cues. Behind them, Isabella and Inspector Satya followed, keeping low and close, their expressions tense as they watched the looming outline of the mansion in the distance, half-obscured by the swirling mist.

The mansion sat atop a cliff, its jagged silhouette framed against the mountainside like a sinister fortress. Its dark windows gleamed faintly in the moonlight, cold and unyielding. Tonight, they would finally breach its walls and face whatever secrets the Order of the Horizon kept hidden within.

As they reached the outer wall, Bijoy raised a hand, signaling the group to halt. He listened, his breath misting in the cold air, and studied the mansion's gate. Two guards patrolled nearby, their voices muffled by the dense fog and soft snowfall.

"Stay close, and move as quietly as you can," Bijoy murmured, his voice barely louder than the whisper of snow on the ground. "Once we're inside, Satya, you stay back to cover the exit. Isabella and I will go deeper."

Pluto sniffed the air, his body taut with anticipation, his ears flattening as he detected the faint scent of gunpowder and oil—a sure sign of more armed men nearby. He let out a low growl, his sharp eyes flicking toward the guards.

Bijoy knelt down, steadying his dog with a gentle hand. "Good boy," he murmured, then glanced back at Isabella and Satya. "On my mark."

They waited, breath held, until the guards passed beyond the gate, disappearing into the shadows cast by the towering mansion walls. Bijoy signaled for them to move, and the group slipped through the iron gate, their movements quick and silent, barely disturbing the snow-covered ground. Satya stayed back, positioning himself near the gate, ready to guard their exit.

They crept along the outer wall of the mansion until they reached a narrow door hidden behind a cluster of ivy. Bijoy pulled the handle, and it opened with a faint creak. He peered inside, finding a dark corridor stretching out into the depths of the building.

"Inside, quickly," he whispered, holding the door open as Isabella slipped past him with Pluto close at her heels.

The air within was stale and cold, filled with the faint scent of musty wood and stone. Shadows danced along the hallway, cast by the flickering light of a single lantern at the far end. Bijoy took the lead, his hand on his pistol as he moved deeper into the mansion, each step careful and deliberate. The walls felt as though they held secrets, watching with an unseen gaze as the intruders slipped through the mansion's innards.

They made their way through the dim corridors, guided only by the occasional beam of moonlight filtering through the

WINDS OF THE SILENT HILLS 23

high, narrow windows. The mansion was eerily quiet, the only sounds the faint hum of the wind outside and the soft echo of their footsteps on the stone floor.

As they rounded a corner, Pluto's ears perked up, and he let out a low growl, his body tense as he stared at a heavy wooden door to their left. Bijoy held up a hand, signaling Isabella to stop.

"There's someone inside," he murmured, his eyes narrowing as he focused on the door. "We'll need to take them out before they can sound the alarm."

He nodded at Isabella, who drew her knife, her face set in determination. With a swift movement, Bijoy opened the door and slipped inside, Pluto right at his side. The room was dimly lit, a crackling fire casting an orange glow over the shelves lined with books and strange artifacts. Two men sat at a table, their voices low as they examined a stack of documents.

Before they could react, Bijoy raised his pistol and fired, the silenced shot piercing the air as the first guard slumped over the table. The second guard leapt to his feet, reaching for his weapon, but Isabella was faster, lunging forward and silencing him with a swift, practiced strike.

They waited, breath held, but no other sounds came from the hallway beyond. Bijoy moved toward the table, quickly rifling through the papers. Maps, coded messages, and symbols of the Order covered the pages, each one detailing some part of the society's operation. But they had no time to investigate further.

A sudden noise echoed from the hallway outside—footsteps and the sharp click of a rifle being cocked. Bijoy motioned for Isabella to hide as he slipped behind the door, his pistol ready. The door creaked open, and two more guards entered, their weapons raised as they scanned the room.

Pluto reacted first, lunging at the nearest guard and clamping his jaws around the man's arm. The guard yelped in pain as Bijoy took advantage of the distraction, firing a shot that took down the second guard instantly. Isabella sprang from her hiding spot, grabbing the guard's rifle and aiming it toward the doorway as more footsteps approached.

"Move! We need to keep pushing forward," Bijoy said, grabbing Pluto by the collar and urging him to release his grip on the guard. They dashed out of the room, plunging deeper into the mansion as the sound of voices and hurried footsteps followed them down the corridor.

The hallways twisted and turned like a labyrinth, each one looking almost identical in the darkness. Their path was illuminated only by the occasional lantern or the faint light of the moon through distant windows. They pressed on, searching for the lower-level chambers they believed held the Order's secrets.

As they rounded another corner, they came face to face with a group of guards emerging from a room at the end of the hallway. There was a split-second pause, both sides frozen in shock, before the air exploded with the thunderous sound of gunfire. Bijoy fired his pistol, taking out one of the guards, while Isabella ducked behind a pillar, returning fire with the rifle she'd taken.

Pluto barked, his powerful frame moving swiftly as he weaved between the guards, biting at ankles, lunging at arms, using his sheer strength and speed to disrupt their formation. The narrow corridor erupted into chaos as guards shouted, trying to aim around the dog's frantic attacks. One guard managed to hit Bijoy's shoulder, the force of the bullet knocking him back against the wall, but he gritted his teeth and fired back, his aim precise.

"Bijoy!" Isabella shouted, her voice tight with fear as she saw the blood seeping through his sleeve.

"I'm fine—keep going!" he called back, barely pausing to reload as he downed another guard. They pushed forward, Pluto leading the way, his growls filling the air as he lunged at anyone who dared to get close to his master.

Finally, they reached a large door at the end of the corridor. Bijoy threw his weight against it, forcing it open. They stumbled inside and slammed the door shut, blocking it with a heavy piece of furniture as they caught their breath.

The room they had entered was vast and dimly lit, filled with crates and stacks of documents. A strange, pungent smell hung in the air, as if something ancient had been left to rot. Isabella pressed her ear against the door, listening to the muffled shouts of the guards regrouping outside.

"Is this... what we came for?" she asked, her voice barely a whisper.

Bijoy's eyes scanned the room, noting the symbols painted on the walls, the strange artifacts scattered across the tables. "We don't have time to check everything, but grab what you can," he said, motioning toward the papers nearest them. "If we can bring some of this back, it'll be enough to expose them."

Isabella nodded, quickly gathering as many documents as she could while Bijoy searched the crates, his hands moving swiftly over the strange objects inside. Pluto remained by his side, his eyes fixed on the door, ready for any sign of movement.

Their respite was brief. A loud crash echoed from outside the door as the guards began to break through. Bijoy grabbed Isabella's arm, pulling her toward a door on the opposite end of the room. "We need to get out of here—now."

They raced through the mansion's maze-like hallways, hearing the pounding footsteps of their pursuers behind them. As they neared the upper floors, Bijoy's mind raced, considering their options. The sounds of the guards grew louder, and he knew they were running out of time.

"Over here!" he whispered, leading Isabella and Pluto toward a small balcony that jutted out from one of the upper corridors. The balcony was exposed to the night air, overlooking the cliffside and the dense forest far below.

Bijoy glanced back, his mind calculating the distance. If they could climb down to the ledge just beneath the balcony, they might be able to slip away down the side of the cliff, disappearing into the forest before the guards could catch up.

But as they neared the edge, a shout went up behind them, and a hail of bullets struck the stone wall, sending shards of rock and dust into the air. Bijoy pushed Isabella ahead, urging her onto the narrow ledge below.

"Go! I'll hold them off!"

Isabella climbed down, gripping the icy stone for balance as she made her way toward the cliffside. Pluto hesitated, his eyes on Bijoy, unwilling to leave his master. Bijoy gave the dog a firm nod, silently urging him to follow Isabella. But just as Pluto began to descend, a guard charged at Bijoy, knocking him back.

Bijoy struggled against his attacker, grappling with him as they neared the edge of the balcony. The guard's grip was strong, his face twisted in rage as he tried to force Bijoy over the edge. With a final surge of strength, Bijoy broke free, shoving the guard aside. But in the chaos, he lost his footing, his body pitching backward as he fell.

For a brief moment, he felt weightless, the freezing night air rushing past him as he plummeted toward the river far below. The roar of the water filled his ears, and he caught a fleeting glimpse of Isabella's horrified face, her mouth open in a silent scream, before the icy river swallowed him whole.

Isabella clung to the cliffside, her heart pounding as she stared at the spot where Bijoy had disappeared into the misty river below. She could barely breathe, her mind numb with shock and grief. Pluto whimpered, leaning over the edge, barking frantically as if calling Bijoy back.

Satya reached her side, his face pale as he took in the empty space below. "Isabella... we have to go. The guards are closing in."

She nodded slowly, her movements mechanical as she tore her gaze from the cliff's edge, following Satya and Pluto down the mountain path. Every step felt heavier than the last, as if a part of her heart had been left behind with Bijoy, lost to the churning waters of the valley.

As they made their way down, she glanced back, her mind racing with a desperate hope. She would search every inch of that riverbank, comb the entire forest if she had to. She wouldn't leave until she knew for certain.

The dawn broke pale and gray over the valley, casting a cold light over the forest as they reached the edge of the river, but there was no sign of him. Only the rushing waters and the vast, empty silence of the mountains remained.

With Pluto at her side, Isabella began her search, her heart heavy with determination, vowing to find Bijoy—no matter how long it took.

Chapter 4: Into the Mist

Isabella's breath clouded in front of her as she trekked down the treacherous mountain path, glancing over her shoulder every few steps. The society was closing in on her—she could feel it as surely as she felt the biting cold through her clothes. The loss of Bijoy weighed on her, his sudden absence a void that seemed to stretch endlessly into the mist that surrounded her. The only solace she found was in knowing that Pluto, faithful and unyielding, had taken off downriver to search for him.

The harsh terrain left her feet sore and her body exhausted. She stumbled over the roots that crossed the narrow mountain paths and over slippery rocks as the fog grew denser, muffling even the sounds of her footsteps. Her breath came in sharp bursts, visible in the freezing air, and her mind raced as she planned her next move. With Bijoy gone and Satya forced to flee in the opposite direction, she was on her own. She had to keep moving, stay one step ahead of the Order's agents, and survive until she could regroup with Satya—or find some new path out of this nightmare.

The sound of snapping twigs to her left made her freeze, her hand instinctively reaching for the knife Bijoy had given her weeks earlier. She crouched, holding her breath, listening intently for any sign of movement in the shadows. But after a moment, the forest returned to its cold, unnatural stillness.

Her hands trembled as she held her knife, her fingers stiff from the cold, her knuckles white against the worn leather handle. She knew they were coming, and with each passing hour, the distance between her and the Order's men grew smaller. The trail she had followed was perilously narrow and barely visible through the mist, but it led away from the main paths and kept her concealed, for now.

The wind picked up, carrying with it the faintest sound of voices—murmurs and shouts distorted by the thick fog. Her heart pounded as she realized how close they were, just out of sight, their forms hidden by the thick autumn mist. She pushed herself forward, ignoring the protests of her aching legs, willing herself to keep going. Her path cut sharply to the left, leading her up a steep incline lined with jagged rocks and loose gravel.

A sense of desperation fueled her steps as she climbed, her hands slipping against the cold, damp stones. As she neared the top, a shout echoed from below, closer this time. She dared a glance back, squinting through the mist to make out dark figures moving along the path she had just left.

Panic surged through her. She scrambled to the top of the incline, her feet sliding against the loose stones as she struggled to pull herself up. She pushed forward blindly, her instincts guiding her as she fled deeper into the mountains, away from the men who pursued her. Her breath came in gasps, each one a desperate plea for escape as the mist closed in around her, shrouding the forest in a gray, suffocating silence.

Hours passed in a blur of exhaustion and fear as she wound her way through the forest, climbing over fallen trees, ducking under low-hanging branches, and weaving through the dense undergrowth. She'd lost any sense of direction, relying solely on her instincts to guide her away from the danger that lurked behind her.

As night fell, the temperature dropped further, the cold seeping through her thin jacket and gnawing at her skin. She shivered violently, her teeth chattering as she searched for shelter. The fog had thickened, settling in a low, impenetrable cloud over the forest, making every tree and rock look like a looming specter. Her breath hung in the air in short, desperate puffs, and she forced herself to keep moving, despite the chill that numbed her fingers and toes.

After what felt like an eternity, she stumbled upon a small rock outcrop that jutted out from the side of a hill, forming a shallow cave. She crawled inside, curling up against the stone as she tried to conserve her body heat. The darkness was absolute, pressing in on her like a weight, and she could barely see her own hand in front of her face. The wind howled outside, a relentless force that seemed to mock her isolation, and the distant sound of footsteps continued to haunt her, reminding her that her pursuers were never far behind.

Her stomach growled, a hollow ache that gnawed at her insides, but she ignored it. She'd rationed what little food she had left, barely enough to sustain her. Sleep was a luxury she couldn't afford, not with the knowledge that they were still out there, scouring the mountainside, their search as unrelenting as the bitter cold. Instead, she sat huddled against the rock, clutching the knife Bijoy had given her, her thoughts consumed by memories of him.

His voice echoed in her mind, steady and reassuring, the way he'd always been when she felt lost or afraid. She could almost feel his presence beside her, his hand on her shoulder, his quiet strength a comforting balm in the midst of chaos. But now he was gone, lost to the river, and she was alone in the vast, unforgiving wilderness, with nothing but the biting wind and the suffocating fog for company.

"Bijoy..." she whispered into the darkness, her voice barely louder than a breath. The word hung in the air, a plea, a hope that somehow, he might still be out there, waiting for her. But the silence that followed was deafening, and she knew that if she was to survive, she would have to rely on her own strength, her own instincts, just as he'd taught her.

Dawn came reluctantly, a pale, colorless light filtering through the fog that clung stubbornly to the trees. Isabella forced herself to her feet, her body stiff and aching from the cold. She was exhausted, every muscle sore, her skin numb from the frigid night. She took a tentative step forward, wincing as pain shot through her legs, but she pushed on, determined to put more distance between herself and the men who pursued her.

The hours blended into each other as she moved through the forest, her senses heightened, every snap of a twig or rustle of leaves setting her heart racing. She was on the brink of exhaustion, her vision blurring as the cold seeped into her bones, and the thought of rest felt like an impossible luxury.

As she stumbled through the undergrowth, she became aware of a faint noise in the distance—the crackling of a fire. Her heart leapt, hope sparking within her, and she followed the sound, her steps cautious, her hand on the knife tucked into her belt.

As she neared the source of the sound, the faint scent of wood smoke filled the air, mingling with the damp, earthy smell of the forest. She moved quietly, peering through the trees until she saw the source of the smoke—a small, makeshift campsite nestled among the trees, with a lone figure crouched beside the fire, his face hidden beneath a hood.

She watched him for a moment, studying his movements, noting the care with which he tended the fire, his hands steady and sure. He didn't look like one of the Order's men—his clothes were worn, his posture relaxed, lacking the rigid discipline she'd come to associate with the society's agents.

Steeling herself, she took a step forward, her voice barely louder than the crackling flames. "Hello?"

The man looked up, his gaze sharp and assessing as he took in her appearance. His face was weathered, lined with the marks of hard years, but his eyes held a warmth that surprised her. He stood slowly, his movements unhurried, and extended a hand in greeting.

"You look like you've been through a storm," he said, his voice rough but kind. "Are you alone?"

Isabella hesitated, her hand still on her knife, but something in his demeanor reassured her. She nodded slowly, taking a step closer to the fire, grateful for its warmth. "I... I got separated from my friends. I'm trying to reach the village, but..."

"Ah, the village is quite a distance from here. These mountains aren't kind to wanderers," he said, gesturing for her to sit by the fire. "I'm Dinesh," he added, a faint smile softening his stern features. "A fellow traveler, like yourself."

Isabella studied him for a moment, trying to gauge his intentions, but exhaustion won out over caution. She lowered herself to the ground beside the fire, feeling its warmth seep into her numb skin, a comfort she hadn't felt in days.

"Thank you," she murmured, unable to hide the relief in her voice. "I don't know what I'd have done if I hadn't found you."

Dinesh nodded, his gaze thoughtful as he watched her, as if assessing her story. "You look like you've been running," he said, his tone cautious. "People don't usually wander these parts without a reason."

Isabella hesitated, her mind racing. She didn't know how much she could trust him, but she sensed that he could see through any lie she might tell. "I... I've been trying to escape the Order of the Horizon," she admitted, her voice barely above a whisper.

Dinesh's expression darkened, and he glanced over his shoulder, as if expecting to see the society's agents materialize from the mist. "They're here, too?" he asked, a trace of anger in his voice.

Isabella nodded. "They... they killed someone close to me. I've been running ever since."

Dinesh was silent for a moment, his gaze distant, as if lost in a memory. "You're not the first to run from them. The Order has a long reach, even here in the mountains," he said, his tone bitter. "But you're safe for now. I'll help you get to the village. We'll keep to the trails they don't know about, paths only locals use."

Relief washed over her, and for the first time since Bijoy's fall, she felt a glimmer of hope. "Thank you," she said, her voice choked with emotion. "I... I don't know how to repay you."

WINDS OF THE SILENT HILLS 35

Dinesh gave her a faint smile, his gaze softening. "Survive. That's repayment enough. And maybe... tell me more about this Order. They've caused me my own share of trouble."

Isabella hesitated, but she saw something in his eyes—a resolve, a shared hatred for the society that had upended her life. She told him of their pursuit, the power they wielded, the way they'd followed her and Bijoy into the mountains, relentless in their quest to silence anyone who stood in their way.

Dinesh listened in silence, his face unreadable, though she noticed his hand clench into a fist as she spoke. When she finished, he looked at her, a new resolve in his eyes. "You're not alone in this, Isabella. The Order may think they hold all the cards, but there are those of us who know their weaknesses."

She nodded, feeling a weight lift from her shoulders. For the first time since Bijoy's disappearance, she felt a sliver of hope—a sense that, perhaps, she could find a way out of this, that she could continue the fight Bijoy had started.

As night fell, they huddled close to the fire, its warmth a fragile comfort against the cold that seeped in from the forest. Dinesh spoke quietly, telling her of hidden paths and mountain trails known only to a few. They planned their route, mapping a path that would lead her away from the society's reach, to a place where she could find refuge.

But even as they spoke, Isabella couldn't shake the feeling that the Order was still out there, watching, waiting, biding their time. She knew that she was far from safe, that the journey ahead would be long and treacherous. Yet, with Dinesh at her side, she felt a renewed determination—a promise to herself, to

Bijoy, that she would survive this, and that one day, she would bring down the Order and finish what they had started.

The fire crackled softly as they fell into a tense silence, their eyes scanning the shadows that danced along the edge of the clearing.

Chapter 5: Trust Amid Danger

They walked through the thickening snowfall, Dinesh leading her along hidden paths that seemed to weave endlessly through the forest. Each step was cautious, and each sound, whether it was a snapping twig or a rustle of leaves, made Isabella's heart race. She still didn't know if she could fully trust Dinesh, but something in his steady gaze and calm demeanor reassured her, calming the fears that prickled at the back of her mind.

Her eyes often drifted to his back as they trudged through the snow, wondering who he truly was beneath his hardened exterior. He walked with a quiet determination, a man who clearly knew these trails well and moved with a confidence born of experience. The silent strength in his posture reminded her of Bijoy, though she quickly pushed the thought away, unwilling to let herself dwell on the painful memories.

Dinesh finally stopped at the base of a hill, his breath misting in front of him as he glanced back at her. "We're almost there. The safehouse is on the other side of this ridge. It's well-hidden; the Order has yet to find it."

Isabella nodded, the cold seeping through her clothes, her fingers numb as she gripped her worn bag. She was too tired to speak, too weary from days of running to even think of forming words. She simply followed him, her footsteps echoing faintly in the vast, snow-covered silence.

Dinesh led her up a winding trail, weaving between thick evergreens dusted with fresh snow. At last, they reached a small clearing, where a rough wooden cabin sat tucked against the hillside, half-hidden by a rocky overhang. The cabin looked simple and rugged, its walls weathered and covered in patches of snow, but a faint plume of smoke rose from its chimney, promising warmth inside.

Dinesh held the door open for her, ushering her in quickly, and she stepped into a room bathed in the glow of a crackling fire. The walls were lined with shelves filled with an assortment of worn books, tin cans, and bundles of dried herbs. A rough wooden table sat near the fireplace, its surface cluttered with maps and papers, and a stack of firewood lay in the corner, ready to feed the flames that warmed the room.

"Make yourself at home," Dinesh said, removing his heavy coat and hanging it on a peg near the door. "It isn't much, but it's safe, and the Order's men rarely venture this deep into the mountains."

Isabella shrugged off her own coat, holding her hands to the fire as she soaked in its warmth. She glanced around, taking in the sparse but cozy room, the faint smell of pine and smoke filling the air. For the first time in days, she felt a sliver of calm settle over her, a fragile peace that she clung to desperately.

Dinesh moved to the table, sifting through a stack of papers as he spoke. "The Order of the Horizon... they're everywhere. They have agents in every city, village, and outpost. I've spent years working against them, gathering a small network of fighters. We're careful, but every step is a risk."

Isabella listened, her mind drifting back to the night of Bijoy's fall, to the cold grip of fear she'd felt as the society's men closed in around them. "You're... part of the resistance, then?" she asked, glancing at him with curiosity and a trace of wariness.

Dinesh nodded, his expression somber. "A small part, yes. It's dangerous work, and the stakes are high, but someone has to stand against them. Too many have lost everything to the Order's grip." His gaze softened as he looked at her, a flicker of understanding in his eyes. "I know that loss isn't new to you."

She lowered her gaze, the weight of grief settling heavily on her shoulders. "My... my fiancé, Bijoy, he was fighting them too," she whispered, her voice barely audible. "We thought we could escape, but... they were relentless."

Dinesh didn't press her for details, and for that, she was grateful. Instead, he simply nodded, as though he understood her pain without needing to hear the full story. "The Order's reach is long, and their power is formidable. But that doesn't mean they can't be defeated. They rely on fear and secrecy to keep their grip on power. Expose them, weaken their hold, and their influence crumbles."

A flicker of hope stirred within her, a faint but stubborn spark. She could see a fierce determination in his eyes, a kind of silent resilience that reminded her of Bijoy's unwavering courage.

Over the next few days, Isabella and Dinesh settled into a steady rhythm, working together to prepare for the resistance's next move. She helped him organize his supplies, tending to the maps and papers he spread out on the table, trying to make sense of the tangled web of connections that made up the Order's network.

It wasn't easy work, and the constant tension of being hunted by the society's agents weighed heavily on her. But she found comfort in Dinesh's presence, his quiet strength a steadying force that helped ease the ache of Bijoy's absence.

One evening, as the snow fell thick and fast outside, Dinesh beckoned her over to the table, his expression thoughtful. "There's something I want to show you," he said, spreading out a worn map. "Our network has a few safehouses scattered throughout the region. Places where the Order's influence is weaker."

He pointed to a spot on the map, a small dot nestled in the valley to the east. "This one here—it's our main base. It's hidden in a network of caves, well-protected, and stocked with supplies. If we can reach it, you'll be safe. And you can meet the others."

Isabella studied the map, noting the winding paths and forested trails that led to the hideout. She felt a surge of hope at the thought of reaching a place where she could finally stop running, even if only for a while. "How long will it take us to get there?"

"With the snowfall, it'll take a few days, maybe more," Dinesh replied, his gaze lingering on the map. "The trails will be treacherous, but we can make it if we're careful."

The next morning, they set out before dawn, trudging through the fresh snow that had blanketed the forest overnight. The air was sharp and crisp, each breath stinging her lungs as they followed the narrow path through the trees. The

WINDS OF THE SILENT HILLS 41

silence was profound, broken only by the occasional snap of a branch underfoot or the distant call of a raven.

As they walked, Isabella found herself growing more comfortable in Dinesh's presence. They exchanged stories of the lives they'd left behind, tales of family and friends, of homes and dreams that had been torn apart by the society's ruthless grip.

"Bijoy would have liked you," she said one evening as they sat around a small fire, the sky above them a dark, endless expanse dotted with stars. "He... he was always drawn to people who fought for something, who believed in a cause."

Dinesh was silent for a moment, staring into the flames, his face cast in shadow. "Sounds like he was a good man," he said finally, his tone soft. "It's men like him who inspire others to keep fighting, even when the odds seem impossible."

She smiled faintly, a pang of bittersweet nostalgia filling her chest. "He was... more than just a good man. He was brave, and stubborn, and he never gave up, no matter how hopeless things seemed."

Dinesh nodded, a faint smile touching his lips. "In that case, let's make sure his fight wasn't in vain."

They fell into a comfortable silence, each lost in their own thoughts as the fire crackled softly, its warmth a fragile shield against the encroaching darkness.

The journey was grueling, each step a battle against the relentless cold and biting wind, but Isabella felt a strange sense of peace settle over her as they walked. She found herself sharing memories of Bijoy with Dinesh, stories of their time together, of the adventures they'd had and the dreams they'd shared. Dinesh listened quietly, his expression thoughtful, his gaze soft with understanding.

One night, as they rested in a small cave tucked into the mountainside, Isabella told him of the night she'd first met Bijoy. "He was so different from anyone I'd ever known," she said, her voice filled with a bittersweet nostalgia. "He had this fire in him, this passion for justice... He believed that even one person could make a difference, that even a single act of kindness could change the world."

Dinesh smiled, his gaze distant. "It sounds like he had a strong spirit, someone who inspired others without even trying."

She nodded, a tear slipping down her cheek. "He did. And I... I want to honor that, to

carry on his fight, even if he isn't here to see it."

Dinesh reached out, gently placing a hand on her shoulder. "You're not alone in this, Isabella. Bijoy's fight is our fight too. We all have a part to play in this."

The words brought a strange sense of comfort, a reassurance that even in her grief, she was not alone. She looked at him, her heart heavy but filled with a newfound resolve. They were no longer strangers bound by circumstance; they were allies, united in a common purpose, and in that shared resolve, she found a strength she hadn't known she possessed.

As they neared the safehouse, a network of hidden caves nestled deep within the valley, Isabella felt a flicker of hope take root in her heart. She knew the journey ahead would be treacherous, that the fight against the Order would test her in ways she could scarcely imagine. But with Dinesh by her side, and the memory of Bijoy's unwavering courage to guide her, she felt ready to face whatever lay ahead.

For the first time since Bijoy's disappearance, Isabella allowed herself to hope—hope for a future free from the Order's grip, hope for a world where people could live without fear. And in that hope, she found a fragile, precious strength that gave her the courage to keep going, one step at a time.

Chapter 6: A New Beginning

The sky was a dim slate, hung heavy with clouds that promised a downpour, and the smell of rain drifted in on a cold wind, sharp and electric. Isabella lay on her bed, her breaths coming short, hands gripping the sheet as the pains started to peak.

Dinesh sat beside her, his face taut and focused, but his hand steady on her shoulder. "She'll be here soon," he murmured, more to himself than to Isabella, as if he needed convincing.

Lightning flashed beyond the shuttered window, and in that brief burst, she saw the raw edge of Dinesh's fear—the crease at his brow and the way his jaw clenched tighter with every one of her cries. Outside, the skies finally tore open, and the rain came down in thick sheets, hammering against the roof and masking their world in a blur of grey.

A midwife, an older woman with silver hair pulled back in a tight bun, stepped forward with a nod. "We're close now," she assured, her voice calm as a lake under winter's ice. "One more push, Isabella."

And with that, a thin wail cut through the thunder and rain. A wail that would forever change them.

The child's skin was a blush of red, her tiny fists clenched as if prepared for a battle. Isabella lay back, exhausted but transfixed, watching the midwife hand the bundle over to Dinesh. He held the child with both hands, staring down at her as if she were something both fragile and infinite.

He looked back at Isabella, his eyes glistening. "We did it. She's here."

Isabella reached out, her fingers brushing the baby's cheek. A warmth surged through her—part joy, part wonder, and something more profound she could barely name. She felt Bijoy's ghost press close, a silent witness to the life he would never know.

The midwife, sensing something unspoken, busied herself at the far end of the room. Isabella wanted to look away from the specter of the past but felt held there, in a gaze she couldn't see but could sense, an invisible pair of eyes watching over her and the child she bore.

With her finger resting on her daughter's tiny hand, Isabella whispered, "Hello, my little one."

The next morning, the rain had quieted to a soft patter, the world outside fresh and bright beneath a hesitant sun. Isabella held her daughter close, feeling her soft breaths, the rhythmic beat of life against her own. But beneath this delicate moment ran a swift, dark current of resolve.

The following evening, with the baby bundled against her chest, Isabella joined Dinesh in the small shed at the village's edge, where the resistance gathered in secret. The walls smelled of damp wood and old rope, and the narrow windows let in only slivers of the twilight.

When Dinesh spoke, his voice was low but fierce. "We're losing ground. Our numbers are thinning, our supplies are short." He glanced around at the others, his gaze lingering on

WINDS OF THE SILENT HILLS 47

Isabella. "But we have hope," he continued, his hand brushing against her shoulder. "And we have a future to fight for now."

The other men and women in the room nodded solemnly, eyes flickering to Isabella and the small bundle in her arms. She felt her cheeks grow warm, realizing the quiet reverence in their gazes wasn't for her alone but for her daughter, their symbol of hope—a living testament to the resilience they were fighting for.

As Dinesh outlined the next stage of their plans, Isabella felt herself grow emboldened. Each word he spoke sank into her bones, melding with her love and fear until they transformed into a steel resolve. For her child, for Bijoy's memory, and for the fragile thread of freedom they grasped at, she would become more than just a quiet supporter. She would become the strength they needed.

Days became weeks, and spring unfurled fully over the village, the rain softening the earth for new growth. Isabella took up training with the other members, her fingers bruised from learning to fire a rifle, her shoulders sore from hours of sparring. But her steps grew surer, her body more resilient.

One afternoon, as she practiced in the woods beyond the village, Isabella heard a whisper, faint and chilling, carried by the wind through the pines. She stopped, her breath caught in her throat, and turned, expecting to see someone standing behind her.

But there was no one—only the forest, shadowed and silent.

"Isabella," the voice had said, familiar yet distant, tinged with longing. She shivered, the memory of Bijoy surfacing with a sudden sharpness. Her heart ached with the love she'd shared with him, the promise they'd built and lost.

Dinesh came to her side, his face pinched in concern. "Are you all right?"

She nodded, brushing off the ghostly sensation, though her pulse still raced. "Just...lost in thought," she murmured.

But the feeling lingered as they walked back together. A part of her wanted to tell Dinesh about the voices, the whispers that pulled her into the past, but she held back. She feared what he might think, and even more, she feared awakening the grief that he, too, bore quietly beneath his sturdy demeanor.

One evening, as they returned from a late meeting, Isabella could feel the weight of Dinesh's silence beside her. The rain had started up again, cool and persistent, blurring the world in a veil of mist.

They walked in silence, the soft slap of rain against cobblestone the only sound between them. Finally, Dinesh spoke, his voice rough, barely audible above the rainfall. "Do you still think of him?"

She felt a jolt, her breath catching in her throat. She had tried to keep her memories of Bijoy hidden, tucked away in the corners of her heart, but Dinesh had seen through her.

She swallowed, feeling the guilt and confusion rise like a wave within her. "I...I can't forget him, Dinesh. But that doesn't mean I don't care about us."

He nodded, though his expression was unreadable in the dim light. "I know," he said, his voice hollow. "But sometimes...I wonder if I'm only a shadow to you, living in a world he built."

The words cut deep, and Isabella felt tears sting her eyes, hidden by the rain. "Dinesh, you're not a shadow. You're my partner, my family." She reached for his hand, but he pulled back slightly, his gaze lost in the rain-slicked street.

They stood there in silence, two figures caught between past and present, as the rain fell around them in a cold, relentless drizzle.

In the dim glow of their small cottage, with their daughter asleep in the corner, Isabella finally turned to Dinesh, the weight of unspoken words pressing on her heart.

She took a deep breath, steadying herself. "I want to tell you everything, Dinesh. About Bijoy. About what he meant to me."

He looked up from his chair, his face weary yet open, a silent invitation for her to speak.

"Bijoy was…he was my first love. But it's more than that." She swallowed, feeling the words knot in her throat. "He was a part of me that I thought I'd lost forever when he died."

Dinesh nodded slowly, a flicker of understanding in his gaze. "And now?"

"Now," she said, her voice soft, "I have a part of him in our daughter. But I also have you, Dinesh. You've given me a second chance. And I want us to build a life together, a future for her."

He looked at her for a long moment, and then, reaching out, he took her hand in his, his

grip warm and sure. "We'll make it work, Isabella. For her. For us."

She squeezed his hand, feeling a swell of gratitude and love. "For us," she repeated.

Outside, the rain had softened to a gentle drizzle, and the world seemed to breathe anew. They sat together in silence, a quiet peace settling over them as they looked toward the promise of dawn.

Chapter 7: Rising Shadows

The evening settled over Ghum like a veil, thick with mist that blurred the sharp edges of the village. Lantern lights dotted the cobblestone pathways, glowing dimly like scattered stars swallowed by the fog. Isabella walked through the village square, feeling the steady weight of her purpose on her shoulders, a purpose that now belonged to more than just herself.

A small crowd had gathered, whispers hushed and tense. Their eyes reflected hope and fear, the shadows of uncertainty casting deep lines on each face. Isabella looked over the villagers, many of them farmers and tradespeople, ordinary souls caught in the extraordinary grip of resistance.

Dinesh stood beside her, his hand a quiet reassurance on her shoulder. He nodded, his eyes steady, urging her forward. She took a deep breath, her gaze sweeping over the crowd as she began to speak.

"Tonight," she began, her voice low but fierce, "we stand together, not as a mere resistance, but as a family—one that stretches across every home, every hearth in this village. The enemy seeks to take away our freedom, but they cannot take away our courage, our will to protect our land, our children."

A murmur of agreement stirred among the listeners. Isabella pressed on, her voice swelling with the conviction that grew within her like fire.

"They may have their weapons, their soldiers, but we have each other. And together, we are stronger than they know."

The crowd's murmurs grew louder, heads nodding, a few fists rising in solidarity. Isabella saw hope bloom in their eyes, their faces softened by a shared sense of purpose. She caught the gaze of an older man standing at the back, a glint of pride mixed with defiance in his eyes, as if she'd reminded him of something he'd thought long buried.

When her voice fell silent, the night itself seemed to pulse with their unified strength. For a brief moment, she allowed herself to feel the pride and power surging through her, knowing that each one of these people stood by her, willing to fight for freedom.

Rain dripped from the eaves as Isabella and Dinesh moved through the backstreets, silent as shadows. The mist hung thick, cloaking them in secrecy as they wove their way to the edge of the village, where the enemy supply routes snaked through the underbrush and over the old stone bridge.

Dinesh's footsteps were light but purposeful, his presence a steadying anchor beside her. As they neared the bridge, he whispered, "Stay close. We don't know how many guards they'll have tonight."

The rain had left the ground slick, and their boots sank softly into the mud as they crouched behind a stack of barrels, their eyes fixed on the approaching convoy. The soft glow of lanterns bobbed down the road, the soldiers' voices a low murmur carried by the breeze.

Isabella glanced at Dinesh, catching the steel in his gaze as he signaled to wait. She felt her pulse quicken, the thrill of danger sparking through her veins. Her hand tightened around the small knife she'd tucked in her belt, its cool edge a reminder of the razor-thin line they walked tonight.

Just as the first wagon rumbled onto the bridge, Dinesh leaned closer, his breath warm against her cheek. "On my count," he murmured. His voice was steady, calm, the voice of a man who had faced danger a thousand times.

"One...two..."

But before he reached three, a soldier turned sharply, his lantern beam sweeping across the shadows, freezing as it caught the glint of metal in Dinesh's hand.

"Who's there?" the soldier barked, stepping forward, his rifle raised.

In a heartbeat, Isabella felt Dinesh pull her to the side, pressing her back against the wall as they flattened themselves against the rough stones. She held her breath, her heart hammering as the soldier's footsteps grew louder, his shadow stretching across the ground.

The sound of the convoy continued, oblivious to the soldier's absence, and for a tense moment, it was only the sound of the soldier's footsteps and the distant hum of the rain. Isabella's grip tightened on her knife, ready to strike if the soldier came any closer.

But then, as if by some unspoken mercy, the soldier's footsteps halted. The shadow turned and retreated, merging back into the fog.

Dinesh exhaled, a small, tense breath, and he squeezed her hand in the silence. She met his gaze, and in that single look, they shared the rawness of the moment—the vulnerability, the fear, and the unspoken bond that had only grown stronger.

"We move now," he whispered, his voice low and fierce.

They darted out from the shadows, slipping past the convoy just as it passed, blending back into the mist as they made their escape.

That night, as the rain whispered against the roof, Isabella lay in the dark, her mind slipping through fragments of memory, shadows that curled around her like the night itself.

She drifted into sleep, and with it, into a vision of Bijoy. He was standing on the edge of the forest, his figure partially hidden in the mist, his face a mixture of sorrow and longing. She reached out to him, her hand trembling as she took a step forward, but he held up a hand, a silent barrier that stilled her.

"Bijoy," she whispered, her voice catching.

He looked at her, his eyes deep with a sadness she could feel resonate through her bones. "Isabella," he said, his voice as familiar as her own heartbeat, "you've chosen your path."

She wanted to tell him about Dinesh, about their daughter, about the life she was building from the ashes of the past. But the words stuck in her throat, and she found herself rooted to the spot, unable to reach him.

Bijoy's gaze softened, and he gave her a nod, as if he understood all that she couldn't say. He stepped back, the mist curling around him until he was nothing more than a shadow against the trees.

When Isabella woke, her face was wet, her breath shallow, as though she'd run miles through the rain. She pressed her hand to her chest, feeling the echo of Bijoy's presence linger, a bittersweet reminder of the life they'd never had.

WINDS OF THE SILENT HILLS

The next afternoon, the rain had ceased, leaving behind a damp, heavy silence. Isabella sat alone in the small attic room, the light filtering in soft and golden. As she moved a stack of old clothes, a corner of paper caught her eye—a letter, yellowed with age, its edges brittle.

Her fingers trembled as she opened it, recognizing Bijoy's handwriting instantly. Each word, each curve of ink, seemed to pull her back in time, to a memory that had waited patiently in the shadows.

Isabella,

If you're reading this, then I may no longer be by your side. But know that my heart has always belonged to you, even if fate has chosen a different path for us. Do not mourn for me, but remember that I am with you, in spirit and in love, as long as you carry our dreams.

Love, Bijoy

The words blurred as her eyes filled, and she pressed the letter to her heart, feeling the echo of his presence like a warmth that seeped through her skin. She felt his love as keenly as the day he'd first confessed it, a part of her life that time and distance could never sever.

The quiet of the attic filled with her grief and her love, a silent testament to all that they'd shared—and all that she'd lost.

That night, Isabella shared the letter with Dinesh, her fingers tracing the delicate edges as she handed it over to him. He read in silence, his face impassive, but she could see the flicker of pain in his eyes as he finished.

"He was…an important part of you," he said softly, his voice rough with understanding.

Isabella nodded, her voice tight. "I think I've been holding on to him, maybe too much. But I don't know how to let him go."

Dinesh took her hands, his grip firm and warm. "Sometimes, it's the hardest thing to do. But maybe it's time to give him a place in the past, so we can build the future we want."

They walked together to the edge of the village, where the forest began, and Isabella placed the letter at the foot of a tall oak tree. She stepped back, feeling a bittersweet ache in her heart as the night wrapped around them, the moon casting a pale glow over the clearing.

In that quiet moment, Isabella felt Bijoy's presence fade, a gentle warmth slipping away like mist at dawn. She held Dinesh's hand, a sense of calm settling over her as they turned back toward the village, ready to embrace the life they'd chosen.

The fog drifted away with them, leaving behind the quiet shadows of the forest and the memory of a love that had shaped her, even as she stepped forward into a new beginning.

Chapter 8: Storm of Ghosts

The air was thick with rain, a torrent that fell from the sky in angry, relentless sheets. The market was half-flooded, with muddy water pooling between the stalls, and merchants huddled beneath makeshift shelters, shouting over the roar of the downpour. Isabella adjusted her shawl, pulling it tighter against the chill as she scanned the crowd.

In the haze of gray, she almost didn't see him. But there, through the throng of people and umbrellas, a figure moved with a familiar gait, shoulders back, head held high. She froze, her heart pounding as she squinted against the rain.

A British officer, his uniform crisp despite the weather, his face shadowed under a wide-brimmed hat—but there was no mistaking it. Beneath the unfamiliar garb, the sharp cheekbones and the slight, almost hidden smile were unmistakable.

Bijoy.

Isabella's breath hitched, her pulse racing as she ducked behind a stall, her eyes locked on him. It couldn't be. Bijoy was dead. She'd mourned him, buried him in her heart, held his memory close. And yet, here he was, weaving through the marketplace as if no time had passed.

Her grip tightened on the edge of a stall, the cold, wet wood biting into her palms. A surge of desperation filled her chest, drowning out all reason. Without another thought, she slipped into the crowd, following the officer at a distance, her steps quick but silent as she fought to keep him in her sight.

The rain lashed against her, soaking through her shawl and dripping into her eyes, but she pressed on. She stayed close, ducking behind barrels and carts whenever he turned, her heartbeat loud in her ears as the distance between them dwindled.

When he reached the edge of the market, he stopped abruptly, looking out toward the mist-covered road that led toward the British encampment on the hill. Isabella hid behind a stack of crates, watching, her breaths shallow, her mind racing. She felt an ache, a fierce longing mixed with anger, her hands clenched tight as she waited, praying he would turn just once, so she could see his face clearly.

But he didn't. The officer stepped forward, his form swallowed by the fog, until he was nothing more than a shadow.

The rain didn't let up, continuing to pour with an almost vengeful force as Isabella made her way back through the flooded streets, her mind a tangle of disbelief and confusion. The image of Bijoy—alive, wearing the uniform of the enemy—haunted her like a fever dream. Each flash of lightning seemed to bring him back, his face ghostly against the stormy sky.

When she reached her small cottage, she shut the door, leaning against it as the sound of the rain pounded on the roof, mirroring the storm raging in her chest. How could he be alive, and wearing that uniform? She had mourned him, mourned the man who had fought beside her, whose heart had been as committed to the cause as her own. And now...had he betrayed it all?

Her thoughts spiraled, memories surfacing in fractured pieces: his fierce loyalty, the promises they'd whispered in the safety of moonlit nights, the words that had bound them to each other. She remembered the conviction in his voice, the fire in his eyes when he spoke of freedom, of his hatred for the British rule.

And now, here he was, one of them.

It didn't make sense. The Bijoy she knew would rather die than betray his people. She paced the room, her heart aching, unable to shake the gnawing feeling of betrayal that twisted within her. The room was dim, lit only by a flickering oil lamp, casting long shadows on the walls, their shapes bending and warping with each step she took.

But a deeper question crept in, one that unsettled her even more than the sight of him in that uniform. Had she truly known Bijoy at all?

The cottage was dim as Isabella returned, the rain tapping against the window, a quiet rhythm that filled the silence between her and Dinesh. He watched her, his brow furrowed with worry, as she sat across from him, her hands clasped tightly in her lap.

She took a deep breath, the words spilling out like water breaching a dam. "I saw him, Dinesh. I saw Bijoy, in the market. He was...he was wearing a British uniform."

Dinesh's face stilled, his eyes darkening as he absorbed her words. His fingers curled, pressing into his palms, but he remained silent, his gaze never leaving hers.

Dinesh's jaw tightened, a flash of hurt crossing his face before he masked it. "And what do you think, Isabella?"

Her hands shook, and she pressed them against her knees, grounding herself. "I don't know what to believe. Bijoy was...he was everything to me. And now, it feels like everything I knew about him was a lie."

The silence that followed was thick, a heavy weight pressing down on them both. Dinesh looked at her, his eyes softening as he reached out, taking her hand in his. "Isabella," he said quietly, his voice filled with an understanding that brought tears to her eyes. "I know how much he meant to you. And I won't ask you to forget him. But I need to know...where do we stand?"

Her gaze dropped to their joined hands, the warmth of his touch a small comfort in the storm raging within her. She felt the pull of her past, of memories she couldn't fully let go, but there, in Dinesh's grasp, was a steadying force, an anchor in the tumult of her heart.

"I don't know how to let go," she whispered, her voice barely audible over the rain.

"But I want to try. With you."

Dinesh's face softened, a faint smile tugging at his lips. "Then that's enough for me."

The rain had begun to pour in earnest, a torrential downpour that blurred the world into a sheet of gray. The rivers had risen, swollen with the monsoon, and the roads were little more than rivers themselves, but Isabella moved through them with a fierce determination, her heart pounding with anticipation and dread.

Her shawl was soaked, clinging to her shoulders, and the icy rain sliced through the air, biting against her skin as she walked toward the outskirts of the village, where the British encampment lay hidden among the hills. Lightning crackled across the sky, illuminating the path before her in harsh bursts, and she used each flash to guide her steps, her resolve steeling with every step.

She felt the weight of her decision settle within her, the knowledge that she was about to confront a part of her life that had defined her, shaped her. If Bijoy had truly betrayed them, if he had chosen survival over loyalty, she needed to hear it from his own lips. Only then could she lay his memory to rest, finally freeing herself to embrace the future with Dinesh.

As she neared the camp, the storm surged, the wind howling through the trees as the rain lashed against her, blurring her vision and numbing her fingers. But she pressed on, her heart a fierce, steady drumbeat in the darkness.

At last, the faint glow of lanterns came into view, illuminating the edges of the camp. She hid in the shadows, her breath shallow as she scanned the faces of the soldiers moving through the camp. And there, standing beneath the dim glow of a lantern, was Bijoy, his face shadowed but unmistakable.

Isabella felt her heart lurch, a mixture of anger and longing flooding through her as she took a step forward, ready to face the man who had once been her everything, now a stranger draped in betrayal.

She called out to him, her voice sharp and clear over the roar of the storm.

"Bijoy."

The word hung in the air, a ghostly echo that cut through the rain, and as he turned, his eyes widened in shock, a flicker of recognition flashing across his face.

The storm swirled around them, a violent tempest that mirrored the storm in her heart, as Isabella prepared to confront the past and demand the truth that had haunted her for so long.

Chapter 9: Shadows of Thunder

The rain poured down in heavy sheets, the world reduced to a watery blur of dark greens and grays, as Isabella followed Bijoy along the forest's edge. Each step she took was weighted with anger, with questions that had no answers, with memories that taunted her heart. The trail was muddy, half-drowned by the downpour, but she barely noticed, her entire focus locked on the man walking just steps ahead.

At last, Bijoy stopped in a small clearing, beneath the jagged canopy of an ancient banyan tree whose thick, twisted branches loomed like silent watchers over their confrontation. His shoulders were tense, his back straight as he turned to face her, the rain carving tracks down his face.

"Isabella," he said, his voice nearly drowned out by the storm.

She clenched her fists, her breath coming in quick, shallow bursts as she struggled to find words that could convey the tumult within her. "Why?" she demanded, her voice sharp as a knife. "Why did you leave us? Why did you join them?"

Bijoy's expression tightened, his eyes flashing with something unreadable, shadowed by the torrent of rain. "You don't understand—"

"You're right," she cut in, her voice rising over the thunder. "I don't understand. The man I loved would never betray his people. Never betray me."

He flinched, a brief look of pain crossing his face before his expression hardened. "I did what I had to. To survive, to…protect you."

The words hung between them, tangled in the storm, and Isabella felt her heart twist, the betrayal so raw, so fresh that she could almost taste it.

"Don't lie to me," she said, her voice trembling. "Not after all we shared. You left me, Bijoy. You left us, and now you're with them. How could you?"

The wind howled through the trees, the rain battering down with an unrelenting force, as if the sky itself demanded the same answers that Isabella sought.

Bijoy's shoulders sagged as he looked down, water dripping from his face, from the edges of his uniform. His voice, when he spoke, was barely louder than a whisper, carried away by the wind.

"They found me," he began, his eyes fixed on the ground. "I was hurt, barely alive. A British patrol discovered me in the forest after that raid. They saved my life, Isabella, but it came at a cost."

She crossed her arms tightly, the sting of anger still fresh. "And that cost was your loyalty?"

He shook his head, a faint, bitter smile on his lips. "They didn't give me much choice. Either I'd rot in their cells, or I'd take the uniform and prove myself useful. I chose to live. For you. For the chance to protect you, even from a distance."

The rain continued to hammer down, cold and merciless, as she listened. Her heart warred with itself, caught between the part of her that longed to believe him and the bitter ache of betrayal that rooted her feet to the wet ground.

"Did you ever think to reach out?" she demanded, her voice shaking. "To tell me that you were alive?"

Bijoy's gaze finally met hers, and in his eyes, she saw the weight of everything he'd endured—fear, regret, and a deep, aching sorrow that mirrored her own. "I couldn't risk it. Not without endangering you. If they suspected I was anything less than loyal, they would have come for you."

Isabella shook her head, wiping the rain from her face as if it could clear away the confusion in her mind. "So you just disappeared? Left me to think you were dead?"

He swallowed hard, a visible pain in his expression as he nodded. "Yes. I thought it was the only way."

The wind surged around them, the trees bending beneath its force, and Isabella felt herself swept up in the storm of his confession. She wanted to believe him, but the betrayal lingered, raw and unhealed.

The sky darkened as thunder rumbled in the distance, rolling like the beat of a war drum. Bijoy's voice softened, almost pleading, as he took a step closer to Isabella.

"Please, understand," he said, his voice hoarse. "I never stopped loving you. I never stopped thinking about you. This uniform...it's a mask, a means to an end. A way to stay close enough to protect you."

Isabella's laugh was sharp, bitter, cutting through the relentless rain. "Protect me? By joining the very people we fought against? By standing alongside them as they trample our land and oppress our people?"

Bijoy's face tightened, and she could see the struggle in his eyes, the weight of his choices pressing down on him. "It was the only way," he said, quieter now, as if convincing himself as much as her. "They would have killed me otherwise. And then you would have had nothing left of me."

She took a step back, the cold mud squelching under her boots. "So you chose this life. You chose them. You chose survival over loyalty."

For a moment, his face crumbled, the mask slipping to reveal a man haunted by regret. "Yes," he whispered, almost inaudible beneath the roar of the storm. "I chose survival. I chose to live, for the faint hope that one day, I might see you again."

Isabella's heart clenched, and she forced herself to look away, the hurt and anger swirling together until she could barely breathe. The storm grew around them, the sky splitting with flashes of lightning that illuminated the tortured expression on Bijoy's face.

But even in his pain, she saw the remnants of the man she'd once loved—the man who had dreamed of freedom, who had stood beside her with a fierceness that she had thought unbreakable. And now, here he was, broken, but alive.

The rain softened slightly, a lull in the storm as Isabella took a steadying breath, her gaze fixed on Bijoy's face. She reached out, her fingers trembling as they brushed his arm, grounding herself in the reality of his presence.

"Bijoy," she said softly, her voice raw with emotion. "Come back. Leave them, leave this...this charade. We can be together, you, me, and our daughter. We can fight for our people, for the freedom we once dreamed of."

His eyes flickered with a spark of hope, but it was gone as quickly as it had appeared, replaced by a look of resignation. He shook his head, stepping back, and the loss of his warmth was like a knife to her heart.

"I can't," he said, his voice hollow. "If I leave, they'll come after me. After you. My position...it's the only thing keeping them from tearing through Ghum, from destroying everything you love."

"But we can fight together," she insisted, her voice rising with desperation. "Dinesh and I, we're building something strong, something worth fighting for. Bijoy, you don't have to do this alone."

He looked away, his gaze lost in the shadowed forest, the sound of the rain mingling with the distant rumble of thunder. "I'm already too far gone, Isabella. I've seen what they do to traitors. If I defect, they'll burn down the village, they'll hunt you down. I won't be the cause of that."

The rain surged again, as if in answer to his refusal, and Isabella felt a sob rise in her throat, the weight of his words settling over her like a final blow.

Isabella stood in the rain, her shoulders shaking as Bijoy's words echoed in her mind. She felt as though the ground beneath her had shattered, leaving her suspended over an abyss. He was choosing them—choosing the uniform, the life that kept him distant and separated from the very people he had once fought beside.

"Goodbye, Isabella," he said, his voice thick with unspoken emotion. He reached out as if to touch her, but his hand hovered in the space between them, the distance as wide as the years they had lost.

She closed her eyes, her heart breaking in a way she hadn't thought possible, and turned away, letting the rain wash over her. Each step she took felt like a farewell, a letting go of everything she had held close, everything she had dreamed of.

As she reached the edge of the clearing, she glanced back once, her gaze meeting his. In that brief, fleeting moment, she saw the man he once was, the man she had loved with every fiber of her being. But that man was gone, lost to a world that no longer belonged to them.

With a final, aching look, she walked away, the rain pouring down like tears from a sky that mourned with her.

The path back to the village was a blur, each step a struggle against the storm that whipped around her, blurring her vision. When she finally reached her cottage, Dinesh was waiting, his face lined with worry as he pulled her inside.

Without a word, she fell into his arms, the warmth of his embrace a balm to her shattered heart. She buried her face against his shoulder, allowing herself to break, to let go of the past that had haunted her for so long.

"I'm here," Dinesh murmured, his voice a steady presence in the darkness. "I'm here, Isabella. And I'm not going anywhere."

And as the storm raged outside, Isabella clung to him, the pain slowly giving way to something softer, a flicker of hope amidst the ruins of her heart. She knew the road ahead would be difficult, but with Dinesh by her side, she felt a spark of strength she hadn't known she possessed.

Together, they would face the future, come what may.

The storm continued to rage, but inside, Isabella felt a quiet calm settle over her. The ghosts of the past had finally been laid to rest, and she was ready—ready to build a life free from shadows, ready to fight for the freedom that she and Dinesh had dedicated themselves to. The rain would pass, and with it, a new dawn would rise.

Chapter 10: The Gathering Storm

Isabella stood at the edge of the village, the last echoes of her confrontation with Bijoy lingering in her mind like a fading storm. She could still feel the weight of his final words, his presence as tangible as the steady drip of rain that fell from the trees. The path ahead was clear now, her heart ached with fresh wounds, but it was steadfast in its purpose.

The air held the faintest scent of wet earth, tinged with the sharpness of monsoon leaves and lingering mist. As she walked back to her cottage, the sky began to clear, thin shafts of sunlight piercing through clouds as they parted, illuminating the small village with a pale glow.

When she opened the door, Dinesh was waiting, his gaze steady but gentle. He looked at her with a mixture of concern and quiet understanding, as if he sensed the weight she carried without needing words. She stepped inside, her face softened with a sad, grateful smile.

"I'm here," she said softly, taking his hand. "For you, for our daughter, for everything we've fought for. I won't look back."

Dinesh squeezed her hand, his expression softening as he reached up to brush a strand of hair from her face. "Whatever happened with him..." he hesitated, choosing his words carefully. "You're still the woman I fell in love with. You're still here, and that's all that matters to me."

The room was filled with a quiet peace, an unspoken promise that wrapped around them like the warmth of the rising sun. Isabella's heart felt lighter, the fog of doubt lifting, leaving behind a raw but steady resolve. She knew now that her path was with Dinesh, with their daughter, with the people of Ghum.

They would fight for freedom, for a world where their daughter could live unafraid.

The rain had softened to a drizzle, a quiet lull that veiled the village in an eerie calm. Isabella was tending to her daughter, her thoughts absorbed in the familiar motions, when a faint knock sounded at the door. Dinesh opened it to reveal a young boy, one of the villagers, his clothes damp and his face tense.

He held out a folded piece of paper, slightly wrinkled from the rain. "This... it's from a British officer. He said it's important."

Isabella took the note, her pulse quickening as she unfolded it. The handwriting was familiar, a sharp pang twisting in her chest as she recognized Bijoy's script.

Isabella,

They're coming for Ghum. Leave while you can. Take Dinesh and the child and go. If you stay, they won't show mercy. I know the consequences of choosing to resist, and I don't want you to suffer them.

Be safe. There is no shame in survival.

Bijoy

She read the words twice, her hands trembling, before looking up at Dinesh. He met her gaze, his brow furrowed as he read the message, a muscle ticking in his jaw.

"They're coming," he said quietly, a fierce determination settling in his eyes. "But we won't run. Not this time."

Isabella folded the note and tucked it into her belt, her face set with resolve. "We've come too far. I won't hide from them. Not now."

Her words rang in the stillness, and for a moment, she thought of Bijoy, his ghost hovering just beyond the edge of her vision. He had warned her, given her a chance to escape, but she knew, in her heart, that running would only delay the inevitable. She could no longer flee from the shadows; she would face them head-on.

With Dinesh by her side, she was ready.

As the clouds thinned, a sense of urgency swept over the village. Isabella and Dinesh moved from door to door, calling upon each villager, gathering them in the clearing under the banyan tree. The old, gnarled branches stretched above them like a protective canopy, shielding them from the misting rain that drifted down in gentle waves.

The villagers were a motley group—farmers, craftsmen, mothers, fathers, young men, and old. They looked at Isabella with trust and expectation, a shared spark that burned in each gaze. She felt a surge of pride mixed with fierce protectiveness as she spoke, her voice strong and clear.

"They're coming to take what's ours," she said, her eyes scanning each face. "Our homes, our freedom, the land we've tilled and tended for generations. But we won't let them. Not today. Not while we can still fight."

A murmur rippled through the crowd, and one by one, the villagers raised their voices in agreement, their resolve solidifying into something unbreakable. An old man stepped forward, his face lined with years but his posture straight and defiant. "You've given us hope, Isabella. And that's something they can't take."

Others followed suit, each one echoing their commitment, their voices blending into a single, resonant sound that filled the air like thunder. Dinesh moved among them, offering words of encouragement, his presence a steady force that lent strength to those around him.

Isabella felt a spark of anticipation, the flicker of a quiet hope igniting within her. Together, they would stand against the storm. Together, they would protect their home.

The afternoon had given way to a subdued twilight, the clouds shifting in shades of deep blue and gray as Isabella made her way to the forest's edge. A sense of finality weighed on her, a pull she couldn't ignore, and as she reached the clearing, she saw him standing there, half-hidden in shadow.

Bijoy looked up as she approached, his face etched with regret. He held his hands at his sides, his stance calm but his eyes stormy with unspoken words.

"You came," he said quietly.

She nodded, her gaze unwavering as she took him in one last time. The pain of their parting still lingered, but it had dulled to a quiet ache, a scar she could carry without flinching. "This is goodbye, Bijoy."

His jaw clenched, and he nodded, the words settling heavily between them. "I wanted to save you, Isabella. To keep you safe."

She stepped closer, the rain a soft patter on the leaves above, and reached out, letting her fingers brush against his arm. "I don't need saving, Bijoy. Not anymore."

For a moment, they stood in silence, each of them carrying the weight of their shared history, the love they'd known and the lives they'd led apart. His hand reached up to cover hers, their fingers entwining in a gesture that felt both familiar and foreign.

"You're brave, Isabella," he murmured. "Braver than I ever was."

She shook her head, a soft smile ghosting over her lips. "I chose my path, Bijoy. Just as you chose yours."

With one final look, they parted hands, the touch lingering like the last wisp of a memory. Isabella stepped back, her heart steady, her purpose unshaken. Bijoy watched her go, his figure fading into the shadows, a ghost of the life she was leaving behind.

As she walked away, the sky began to clear, a thin strip of light breaking through the clouds, illuminating the path before her. She felt a quiet sense of closure, a resolve that settled into her bones. This was her journey now, her fight.

And she was ready to face it.

The sun had barely risen the next morning when the first sign of the approaching assault reached them. A scout returned, breathless and soaked, his face drawn as he relayed the news.

"They're coming," he said, his voice a hoarse whisper. "The British—dozens of them. Armed and ready."

A chill settled over the village, a silence thick with anticipation as Isabella gathered the villagers, each face etched with a mixture of fear and determination. She stood at the center, her voice calm and steady, her heart fierce with the will to protect.

"We've trained for this," she said, her voice carrying over the crowd. "We've prepared. Now we stand together, not just as villagers but as fighters. This is our land, our home. We won't let them take it from us."

Dinesh joined her, his gaze steady as he nodded to those gathered. "They'll try to break us, to scare us. But if we stand firm, if we fight with all we have, they'll find that we're not so easily defeated."

The villagers rallied, their resolve sharpening with each word. The women armed themselves with makeshift weapons, the men gathered supplies, and the younger ones set traps along the forest path. There was no longer any hesitation, only a unified determination that pulsed through the village like the beat of a war drum.

As they worked, the sky grew darker, clouds gathering once more, the rumble of distant thunder signaling the coming storm. Isabella felt the energy thrumming in the air, her pulse quickening as the final preparations were made.

In the hours that followed, she moved among them, offering words of encouragement, her presence a quiet strength that steadied even the youngest among them. The weight of leadership settled comfortably on her shoulders, and for the first time, she felt fully ready to bear it.

Dusk fell, casting a muted light over the village as they took their positions. The British forces were visible now, their uniforms stark against the trees as they advanced, rifles gleaming in the dim light. Isabella stood at the front, her heart steady, her gaze fixed on the enemy as they closed in.

Beside her, Dinesh took her hand, his grip warm and reassuring. "We'll face this together."

She nodded, a fierce light in her eyes. "For Ghum. For our daughter. For freedom."

As the first shots rang out, the rain began to fall once more, a relentless downpour that mixed with the cries of battle, the thunderous skies mirroring the fierce resolve of those who fought below.

Isabella raised her arm, signaling the resistance forward, her voice rising above the clash and chaos. They charged, a single, unbroken line of courage against the storm, their spirits unyielding as they fought for the lives they'd chosen, for the future they would forge.

And in the heart of the tempest, Isabella found herself—brave, unbreakable, and free.

Chapter 11: The Tempest's Fury

A clap of thunder cracked across the sky as the villagers huddled under the eaves of the banyan tree, the wind tearing through the branches above like a warning. The air felt charged, tense, carrying with it the smell of wet earth and rain. Isabella and Dinesh moved among the crowd, their faces set and determined, their voices rising above the sound of the gathering storm.

"This is our chance to stand strong," Dinesh called out, his gaze sweeping over the faces of the men and women before him. "We fight for our homes, our families. We've prepared for this. Now we just need to hold our ground."

Isabella nodded, the weight of her resolve pressing down like the sky itself. "Remember, we're not alone," she added, her voice fierce. "Every one of us stands together, and together, we're stronger than they could ever imagine."

She glanced around, meeting the eyes of the villagers—her neighbors, her friends, and, in a sense, her family. She saw a flicker of fear in their faces, but more than that, she saw strength, a fierce courage that bound them all. The storm rolled above, dark clouds swirling in a thick mass as they took their places, preparing for the inevitable clash.

Dinesh moved closer to her, his face lit by a flash of lightning that arced across the sky. "Are you ready?" he asked quietly, his voice barely audible over the rumbling thunder.

Isabella's jaw tightened, and she felt her pulse quicken. "More than ever."

The wind howled through the trees, carrying with it the faint sound of marching footsteps, of voices growing louder. The British were coming, and with them, the weight of everything Isabella and Dinesh had fought to protect. She felt her heart beat in time with the storm, steady and fierce, ready for whatever lay ahead.

The first shots rang out, cutting through the roar of the thunder like cracks of lightning, and chaos erupted at the edge of the village. Isabella moved quickly, dodging between trees, her rifle clutched tightly in her hands as she peered through the haze of rain and smoke. The world was a blur of shadows, flickering light, and the flash of gunfire illuminating the night like a twisted dance of fireflies.

The British soldiers advanced in disciplined ranks, their faces obscured by the shadows of their helmets and the storm. Isabella gritted her teeth, her heart pounding as she took aim and fired, the recoil jarring her shoulder as she saw one of the soldiers stumble and fall. Around her, the villagers fought with fierce determination, holding their ground against the tide of redcoats that threatened to engulf them.

"Isabella, to the left!" a voice called out, and she turned just in time to see a British soldier charging toward her, bayonet fixed. She sidestepped, raising her rifle and meeting him head-on. Her movements were quick, efficient, a fluid rhythm she had drilled into herself over countless nights of practice.

The clash of steel and thunder filled the air as she blocked and countered, each movement fueled by a burning resolve that surged within her like a second heartbeat. The rain poured down, slicking the ground with mud and blood, but she held firm, her mind focused only on the next move, the next breath.

In the distance, she could make out Dinesh's figure, moving through the melee with the calm precision of a veteran, his eyes sharp and calculating as he directed the villagers, rallying them with every word. He was a steady presence amid the chaos, a reminder of the strength they held together.

Isabella took a breath, the air thick with smoke and the coppery tang of blood. She had no time to think beyond the moment, beyond the figure before her, the enemy she could see—but little did she know that just beyond the thick curtain of rain, Bijoy fought as well, moving as part of the enemy force that now bore down upon her home.

The British regrouped, the line tightening as they pressed forward with renewed force. The villagers retreated into the heart of the village, forming a barricade of overturned carts and barrels, their faces drawn but unyielding. The sky above was a roiling mass of clouds, heavy with the weight of the storm, and lightning crackled across the heavens as if marking the fury below.

Bijoy moved at the head of one division, his face set and unreadable as he scanned the line of defense, his orders sharp and precise. He pushed down the conflict within him, the pain that twisted his heart with each step closer to the village he had once called home. But duty demanded his loyalty, and he could not afford to falter now.

Unaware of Bijoy's presence, Isabella held her position, her eyes sharp as she aimed across the barricade, her gaze unwavering. "They're closing in," she called to Dinesh, her voice barely carrying over the storm. "We need to hold this line."

Dinesh nodded, a grim determination in his eyes. "We won't let them through," he replied, and together, they rallied the villagers, each one steeling themselves for the final stand.

The British charged, and the clash was immediate and violent. Gunfire and steel met in a thunderous cacophony, each blow echoed by the heavens above. Isabella fired, each shot a prayer, a promise, a vow to protect the lives she had committed herself to.

As she reloaded, she caught a glimpse of a figure leading the charge, his movements precise, relentless, as he urged his men forward. There was something familiar in his stance, a pang that struck her heart, but the battlefield gave no time for questions, no space for recognition.

Around her, the resistance fought with desperate valor, the villagers holding their own as they pushed back against the British line. The rain intensified, falling in sheets that blurred the world, but she kept fighting, kept moving, her purpose clear and unshakeable.

The storm had reached its peak, a furious gale that whipped through the village, flattening crops and tearing at trees. The rain was a relentless torrent, reducing visibility to mere feet, but Isabella pressed forward, her resolve sharpening with every step.

"Now!" she shouted, signaling the villagers who had gathered around her, their faces set with a fierce determination that matched her own. Together, they surged forward, breaking through the barricade with a collective cry that rose above the storm.

The British troops faltered, their ranks thrown into disarray as the resistance surged forward, breaking their formation with a flurry of blows and gunfire. Isabella fought with a fury she hadn't known she possessed, her heart pounding with each swing, each shot. Her movements were swift, instinctive, and she could feel the resistance gaining ground, inch by precious inch.

Around her, the villagers fought with equal ferocity, pushing back the British line as they claimed the village street by street. She caught glimpses of familiar faces—friends, neighbors, all fighting with the same resolve, the same unbreakable spirit.

Dinesh joined her, his eyes alight with pride and determination. "We're pushing them back!"

Isabella nodded, her chest heaving as she took in the sight of their progress. For the first time, victory felt within reach, a glimmer of hope shining through the storm.

Together, they pressed forward, their shouts mingling with the thunder, the rain pounding down in a relentless rhythm as they fought for every inch of their home. The British troops began to retreat, their line broken, and for a brief, precious moment, the village was theirs again.

The storm had begun to abate, the rain softening to a steady drizzle as the last echoes of gunfire faded into silence. The village lay in ruins, the streets littered with debris, the ground churned to mud by the weight of countless footsteps. The sky above was a dim, muted gray, the clouds hanging low as if in mourning.

Isabella walked through the battlefield, her steps slow and heavy as she took in the scene around her. The villagers were moving among the fallen, tending to the wounded, their faces etched with the exhaustion and sorrow that came with survival.

Her gaze swept over the bodies, the silent, still figures that lay scattered like shadows of a battle fought and lost. She paused, her breath catching as she recognized the familiar uniform, the body lying crumpled in the mud.

It was Bijoy.

A cold numbness spread through her as she knelt beside him, her hands trembling as she reached out, brushing a strand of wet hair from his face. His eyes were closed, his features softened in death, as if the battle had stripped away the weight he had carried in life.

A sob escaped her, raw and unbidden, as she traced the lines of his face, the face she had once known better than her own. The memories came rushing back, fragments of a love that had been both fierce and fleeting, a love that had shaped her even as it had torn her apart.

She sat there, the rain mingling with her tears as she grieved, her heart breaking for the man he had been, for the life they had never had, for the choices that had led them both to this final, inevitable end.

Dinesh found her, his expression somber as he knelt beside her, his hand resting on her shoulder in a gesture of silent support. She looked up at him, her eyes filled with a sorrow he understood all too well, and in that moment, words felt unnecessary.

Together, they rose, leaving Bijoy to rest among the fallen, a ghost of the past that had finally found peace.

As they walked back to the village, the rain began to ease, the clouds parting to reveal a pale strip of sky on the horizon. It was a quiet, fragile beauty, a glimpse of hope after the storm, and Isabella felt a faint, flickering warmth in her chest.

The battle was over, but the fight for freedom was just beginning. And with Dinesh by her side, she was ready to face whatever lay ahead, carrying the memory of the man she had loved and lost, and the strength of the family they would build in his honor.

Chapter 12: Shadows of Sacrifice

The pale light of dawn crept slowly over the village, a hazy, ghostly glow that turned the wreckage into something half-seen, a shadowed memory of the lives torn apart. Thick mist hung in the air, swirling softly around Isabella as she moved through the debris-strewn street, her gaze scanning the faces of the villagers, searching desperately for a small, familiar figure.

Smoke rose from the smoldering ruins of huts and carts, mixing with the scent of damp earth and rain. The battle had left scars on the village, on the people, and as Isabella walked past the wounded and the dead, she felt the weight of every step pressing into her chest.

She found Dinesh by the edge of the clearing, his face drawn and weary as he knelt by a wounded man, speaking in low, reassuring tones. He looked up as she approached, a flicker of pain and understanding in his eyes as he reached out to her.

"Is she safe?" he asked, his voice barely above a whisper, thick with worry.

Isabella shook her head, her eyes wide and frantic. "I haven't seen her yet. I have to find her, Dinesh. I have to say goodbye."

He rose, his hand resting on her shoulder as he nodded, his gaze steady despite the sadness that shadowed his face. "Go, then. I'll keep watch."

With a brief, shared look, they parted, Dinesh disappearing back into the mist as Isabella turned, her steps quickening as she searched, her heart pounding with a sense of urgency she couldn't ignore. She moved through the crowd, calling out her daughter's name, each unanswered cry a dagger that twisted deeper into her heart.

The mist wrapped around her like a shroud, obscuring her vision as she pressed forward, driven by a desperation that blocked out everything else. She knew time was slipping through her fingers, that each minute brought her closer to the inevitable, but she had to see her daughter, to hold her one last time.

And somewhere, beyond the haze of smoke and the low murmur of voices, she heard a faint cry—a voice she would have recognized anywhere.

Isabella ran toward the sound, her heart pounding as she pushed through the mist, until at last, she saw her daughter's small figure standing by the remnants of their home, her tiny face streaked with dirt and tears. Her daughter's eyes widened as she saw Isabella, and she ran forward, her arms reaching up in a gesture that was both innocent and heart-wrenching.

"Mama!" the little girl cried, her voice muffled as she buried her face against Isabella's shoulder, clutching her tightly as if she could hold back the world.

Isabella knelt, her arms wrapping around her daughter, breathing in the familiar scent of her hair, her warmth, her life. She blinked back tears, forcing herself to stay strong as she reached into the pocket of her coat and pulled out a small silver medallion—an heirloom she'd carried since her youth.

She slipped the medallion into her daughter's small hand, her voice soft, yet firm. "Hold onto this, my love," she whispered, brushing her fingers over her daughter's knuckles. "I promise you, we'll see each other again. No matter where I am, no matter how far... I will always come back to you."

Her daughter looked up at her, wide-eyed, clutching the medallion as if it were a lifeline, her lips trembling with words she didn't yet know how to say. Isabella pressed a gentle kiss to her forehead, her fingers tracing the lines of her face as if memorizing every detail, storing it away in the quiet corners of her heart.

"Mama?" her daughter asked, her voice barely a whisper, and Isabella could feel the raw, aching pain behind the simple word, the unspoken question that hung between them.

She swallowed hard, giving her daughter a gentle smile, though her heart felt as if it were splintering with each second. "Be brave for me, my little one," she said softly. "And know that I love you, more than anything."

With a final, trembling kiss, she pulled back, meeting her daughter's tear-filled gaze one last time. Then, summoning every ounce of strength she had, she turned away, the mist swallowing her daughter's small figure as she walked back toward the clearing, her heart heavy with the weight of her promise.

A harsh shout cut through the mist, and Isabella's head snapped up to see the unmistakable red uniforms of British soldiers advancing through the village, their bayonets gleaming in the faint morning light. They moved with swift precision, gathering the villagers with practiced efficiency, their faces cold and impassive.

Isabella's pulse quickened as she caught sight of Dinesh, his hands bound behind his back, a soldier at each side gripping his arms. His eyes met hers across the distance, and she felt a pang of fear tighten in her chest. She moved toward him, only to be stopped by the sharp, raised bayonet of a British officer who stepped into her path.

She held her ground, her gaze never wavering as she looked past the soldier, her eyes locked on Dinesh. His expression was one of sorrow but also of quiet resignation, as if he had long accepted the fate that awaited them. He straightened, standing tall despite the bonds that held him, and nodded once, a silent acknowledgment of the path they had chosen together.

For a brief, agonizing moment, neither of them spoke, their silence charged with the weight of unspoken promises, of dreams left unfinished, of a love that had endured even in the darkest of times. Isabella held his gaze, her heart aching as she tried to imprint his face on her memory, to carry it with her wherever they were about to be taken.

The soldiers tightened their grip, pulling Dinesh back as he managed a faint, reassuring smile, his voice barely carrying over the distance. "Stay strong, Isabella. For her. For Ghum."

She nodded, her throat tight, her hand pressed over her heart as she whispered, "Always."

With that final, sorrowful look, they were separated, led away by the soldiers who marched with heavy steps, their bayonets glinting coldly against the misty morning light. Isabella felt the distance between them stretch wider with each step, her heart splintering with the knowledge that she might never see him again.

Rough hands seized Isabella, binding her wrists with a coarse rope as she was pulled through the crowd of villagers, their faces pale and tense in the dim light. She barely noticed the soldiers' grip, her thoughts still lingering on her daughter, on Dinesh, on the village she had fought to protect.

The mist hung thick over Ghum, softening the edges of the broken huts, the charred remains of homes, the faces of the people she had come to love. She felt the rain begin to fall again, a slow, steady drizzle that soaked through her clothes, mingling with the sweat and blood that still clung to her skin.

The soldiers led her to a waiting army truck, its dark, hulking shape barely visible through the veil of mist. They pushed her forward, the jarring movement breaking her reverie, and she stumbled, catching herself as she climbed into the back of the truck, her wrists bound tightly in front of her.

As the engine rumbled to life, she turned, her gaze fixed on the village as it receded into the distance, swallowed by the mist. The faces of the villagers blurred into shadows, their forms melting into the gray morning as the truck moved down the narrow, winding road that led away from Ghum.

Her heart felt heavy, her mind filled with the memories of the life she had built, the love she had found, the daughter she had left behind. She closed her eyes, clinging to the image of her daughter's small hand clutching the medallion, the whispered promise she had made—a promise that bound her as surely as the ropes that held her now.

The mist grew thicker, obscuring the world around her, and as the truck rolled on, Isabella felt a strange sense of calm settle over her, a quiet acceptance of the path she had chosen, of the sacrifices she had made. She would face whatever lay ahead, her heart tethered to Ghum, to the life she had loved and the hope she still carried.

Epilogue

The morning mist thickened, swallowing the village in a suffocating silence, broken only by the distant rumble of engines and the sharp commands of soldiers. Aria, the young daughter of Isabella, stood at the edge of the clearing, the silver medallion her mother had given her clutched tightly in her small, trembling hand. The metal was cold and unyielding, a painful echo of the grief that had anchored in her heart since the soldiers had taken Isabella away.

She peered through the dense fog, her eyes straining to hold onto the final sight of her mother's silhouette as it disappeared into the back of the army truck. Rain coursed down her cheeks, mingling with the tears that threatened to spill, and in an instant, the truck was gone, swallowed by the mist, leaving only the fading roar of its engine.

A shudder ran through Aria, and the medallion in her grasp felt impossibly heavy, pulling her deeper into the clearing. Around her, the battlefield stretched in a mournful sprawl—a chaotic mix of shattered weapons and still bodies that told the story of their defeat. The scent of blood and wet earth thickened the air, pressing down on her as if to suffocate any last glimmer of hope.

The child's feet moved instinctively, the medallion's faint warmth guiding her steps. Her bare toes brushed against something cold and unyielding, and she stumbled, gasping as she fell to her knees. Beneath her lay a body, face turned to the rain, eyes closed in a peace that did not match the violence of his end. His hand was outstretched, fingers curled as if reaching for something he never found.

Aria's breath caught, and her gaze swept over the man's features. Though she didn't know him by name, something in the rugged lines of his face stirred a memory, a story she had overheard whispered among the adults on long, restless nights—stories of a man who stood by Isabella's side, a man named Bijoy. He had been fierce and kind, a protector of the village whose loyalty was unquestioned.

An inexplicable pull kept Aria rooted beside him, her fingers brushing his cold hand, the medallion pressed between them. For a fleeting moment, she thought she felt a warmth, a heartbeat beneath the storm, but it vanished almost as soon as it appeared. Her wide eyes searched his face, not with recognition, but with an instinctual understanding that this loss was deep, shared. This man, unknown to her, had fought for them all.

"Aria!" The shout from a villager broke through the rain, urgent and strained. "Hide, child! They will come back!"

Aria's head snapped up, but her fingers lingered on Bijoy's arm, an inexplicable instinct anchoring her there. The medallion pulsed once more, a bright, silvery light casting a brief glow over his face. Those few villagers who saw it exchanged glances, whispers of confusion and awe cutting through their fear.

The deep rumble of thunder rolled over the clearing, like the growl of an awakening giant. At the edge of the trees, a shadow moved, sharp and deliberate. Aria's eyes darted to it, catching sight of a cloaked figure watching from beneath the dripping branches. Their eyes, dark and intense, seemed to narrow when they met hers, recognizing the gleam of the medallion.

The figure stood unmoving, gaze unreadable but intent. The medallion's glow dimmed, but Aria felt a shiver race down her spine, as though something larger than herself had marked this moment. Behind her, the villagers fell silent, torn between urgency and the haunting sight before them.

The rain came faster, streaking Bijoy's lifeless face, erasing the last signs of battle but not the memory of what he had stood for. A wind whispered through the clearing, carrying a promise Aria could not fully grasp but felt in the marrow of her bones: *Your path is not over, and neither is hers.*

With a final glance at Bijoy, Aria stood, legs trembling but head lifting with a resolve beyond her years. Somewhere beyond the clearing, the engines roared again, signaling the empire's victory and the road that still held her mother captive. The medallion warmed in her hand, steady and insistent, anchoring her as she took a step back.

The cloaked figure lingered a moment longer before melting into the forest, a silent promise echoing in the space between heartbeats. The whispers among the villagers grew louder, uncertain but weighted with a new kind of hope.

Aria turned, eyes still glistening, and looked toward the road where Isabella had been taken. The fight was far from over.

Biswajit Paria is an author known for captivating historical fiction and crime thrillers. His works blend themes of love, betrayal, and resilience set against India's colonial past. His latest novel, Winds of the Silent Hills, set in 1943 in the mountain village of Ghum, follows Isabella and her allies as they face British forces and a secret society, creating an intense journey of survival and sacrifice.

Don't miss out!

Visit the website below and you can sign up to receive emails whenever Biswajit Paria publishes a new book. There's no charge and no obligation.

https://books2read.com/r/B-A-CWOKC-OVZFF

BOOKS 2 READ

Connecting independent readers to independent writers.

Also by Biswajit Paria

The Silent Echoes Series
Winds of the Silent Hills

Standalone
A Letter Never Delivered
Whispers of an Endless Love
The Silent Messenger